Big Red

T. MARTIN KOLLER

DORRANCE
PUBLISHING CO
EST. 1920
PITTSBURGH, PENNSYLVANIA 15238

Dorrance Publishing Co
585 Alpha Drive
Suite 103
Pittsburgh, PA 15238
Visit our website at *www.dorrancebookstore.com*

ISBN: 979-8-88683-294-5
eISBN: 979-8-88683-688-2

Big Red

T. MARTIN KOLLER

CHAPTER ONE

"Examined suspect Karl the talking Rottweiler and have certified the product is not a viable security threat. Karl's computer chip containing speech and movement commands in eighty-six vocalizations in bad English, manufactured in India, shipped to China for assembly, and exported to the United States on the attached invoice date. Port of entry: Oakland, California. The distributor G-L Toys Limited. A random analysis of shipment lots for Karl, show no cryptic or imbedded vocabulary or repetitious content that would lead this agent to believe the product is a vehicle for subliminal messaging as a means of covert communication between terrorist sleeper cells in the United States.

"End of narrative. Agent Frank Kelly. Homeland Security Product Division."

Kelly zipped the report off to Washington.

"Bad English?" Billy Paul commented, sitting like a pot-bellied elf on the other side of a toy-laden workbench. "You realize they're gonna kick it back."

It had been a long day fighting terrorism.

"I doubt they even read our stuff."

Kelly enjoyed the hubris.

Billy Paul, his partner in hubris, stuffed an imported Chinese remote-control helicopter back in its box and slid off his stool.

"Whataya say we grab a couple beers and something to eat, pal."

"This time a night?"

"Barney's got that Gut-Quencher."

"The Board of Health closed that down. Rats, wasn't it?"

"Nah—just a couple roaches." Billy Paul checked his watch. "We haven't been to Barneys in a while."

"Wonder why."

"Shit. It's the only place open for twenty bucks this time a night."

Kelly snatched a windbreaker from the back of his chair as Billy Paul headed for the door.

"Alright, it's Barney's." Kelly flipped off the lights on his way out when he noticed the two red eyes glowing back at him in the dark.

"Whataya know. Karl's a night light, too."

*   *   *

A freezing rain pelted Kelly's black leather jacket as he got out of his Suburban.

This part of Seattle wasn't known for its fine dining. A neglected two-star hotel stood between a row of empty storefronts of a once prosperous neighborhood now gone bad; its flickering red neon sign more a warning than an invitation on a night colder than most in Seattle. The streetlights warned of sleet.

Barneys was half a street away lit up like a cheap carnival.

"Let's go Charlie Brown—it's gettin' nasty!" Billy Paul complained, hunched over against the rain as he made a dash for the lounge's fake medieval doors.

Kelly's Ultra sounded a cavalry charge as he entered Barney's. It was his boss: Peter J. Chapman, Deputy Secretary of Homeland Security.

"You gotta be kidding me," he said, tempted not answering it. "Kelly here!"

"We had an incident in Chicago."

"We?"

"Shut up and listen. It involves a DreamQwest product."

"The gaming company."

"A federal prosecutor in Chicago was wearing one when they found her."

"There's just one problem, boss."

"What's that?"

"It's a domestic. We're federal. Can't touch it."

"It's been approved. You're to go to Chicago and pick it up first thing tomorrow. Your contact is FBI Agent Farris. You'll sign for it and bring it to me personally. Understood? Ticket and details are on your Ultra."

The call ended.

Kelly brushed off specks of sleet from his jacket like so much dandruff as Billy Paul started for the bar, slapping a cigar between his thin lips.

"What Chapman want?"

"A federal prosecutor was found dead in Chicago wearing a Big Red. The boss wants me to take it to Homeland in the morning."

"Sorry, Pal. We don't do domestics."

"He's making an exception."

They bellied up to a near-empty bar with its usual display of whiskey, gin, and wine against a mirror so dirty it distorted their faces like some 50's funhouse. At the other end of the bar was a drunk in a suit trying to drown himself in a shot glass.

"If Chapman asked you to milk a goat," said Billy Paul, lighting his cigar. "You'd be the first one to put on rubber gloves."

"Like you'd say no—right?"

Billy Paul pulled the cigar out of his mouth. "Why you lookin' at me like that?"

"What about the time—?"

"Okay, pal. I get it!"

"Look. The only thing you need to know is you're in charge until I get back."

"It's an illegal product, pal. Your ass is gonna wind up in Kansas."

"You mean Levenworth."

"You think he's gonna save your ass when the shit hits the fan?"

Seattle was Product Division's west coast regional office. Far from being state-of-the-art, it had two laptops and a chip reader. Whoever thought Product Division was anything more than a political clearing house overestimated its role.

The expansion of Product Division grew out of an incident in Europe some years back when German intelligence discovered a batch of electronics from Pakistan with what they thought were instructions directed at terrorist sleeper cells in the Federal Republic. That, in turn, gave rise to a new division within the Department of Homeland Security; the idea being that if it could happen in Germany, it could happen in the United States as well.

"Where the hell's Buster?" Billy Paul cursed, gnawing on his cigar.

A small impish man with wirey white hair and a red leather vest popped up from behind the bar.

"Hey—!"

"Christ's sake, Buster. What the hell were you doin' back there?"

"In the basement. Beer inventory."

Kelly looked at his partner. "You realize he heard every word we said."

"Yeah."

"Now we'll have to kill him."

Buster's eyes widened. "Honest guys. I was just—"

"We gotta have our beer first," Billy Paul laughed. "Maybe later."

"You were kiddin'—right?"

The interior of Barney's was a cheap replica of a medieval castle complete with fake colonnades. A plaintiff Irish ballad played in obvious contradiction to an English coat-of-arms hanging above a fake stone fireplace.

"Where's everybody by the way?"

"I sent 'em home—slow night," said Buster.

Kelly slapped a twenty on the bar and climbed up onto a peeling red-leather stool. "I'll take a Sam Adams."

Billy Paul ordered a draft.

"Only cops drink outta mugs," the drunk at the other end of the bar stammered, raising an empty shot glass.

Buster ignored him.

"And two gut quenchers," Billy Paul added, slapping down a ten note like a winning ace in a close card game.

"Sorry, B-P. Kitchens closed. All I got is pretzels and peanuts," he said looking up at the clock. "I'll be closing in an hour."

A Sam Adams and a draft were served up along with two bags of peanuts. Billy Paul emptied one bag himself. "So, what's the plan, Chemo savvy?"

Kelly took a long swig of his Sam Adams. "Certify the obvious and concentrate on the priorities until I get back."

"They're *all* priorities this time of year."

"Do what you can."

A few years ago, there were four Product Division regional offices in the United States: New York, Chicago, Galveston, and Seattle: all port cities.

That was before the cuts in personnel.

Vacancies that were never filled. New York and Seattle were the only two surviving. On the government's totem pole, Product Division was somewhere at the bottom along with Fish and Game.

It had been pointed out in Senate hearings that checking every toy and gadget entering the United States was tantamount to looking for a square peg for a round hole. Statistics was what was killing Product Division.

Statistics were the meat and potatoes of politics. It justified budgets, along with careers. Ironically, Product Division had yet to find a single suspicious imported gadget, let alone a potential terrorist threat.

Statistics worked both ways.

Political supporters of a particular government program, in this case Product Division, could say it was batting a thousand, while opponents could say there was no threat to begin with.

Kelly had long ago concluded Product Division was nothing more than a placebo; something to show a fearful public the government was doing its job. It paid the bills. Why complain?

"How long have we been doing this, B-P?"

"Drinkin' beer?"

"Never mind."

His partner rolled a ball of smoke off his tongue. "Our job's like digging holes in the sand with a spoon, pal."

"What's your point?"

"All we do is put our stamp of approval on a bunch of toys. What if next time we get a nuke?"

"It would have to be a pretty damned small nuke, B-P."

Billy Paul cackled a response as he always did to a bad joke.

"By the way. How's Robby?" said Kelly, realizing too late his mistake. It wasn't something he wanted to talk about over beer.

His partner pulled the cigar from his mouth and stared up at some imaginary spot on the ceiling. "Not much better."

"Hey, look—"

"Last time I checked," said Billy Paul, "his therapist told me he's got some feelin' back in his right leg," glancing over at Kelly. "A lot better now than he was a year ago when all he could do was open and close his eyes."

Army Lieutenant Robert Paul Stevens' Mountain Division, sent to Afghanistan during Operation Clean Sweep in 2026 as part of the Pentagon's new war strategy in central Asia along with 120,000 Marines and Special Forces personnel including NATO allies.

An old war with a new name.

Less than a week after arriving at Bagram Air Base, Billy Paul's son was torn apart by an I-E-D on a one-man goat trail in a rugged mountain region near the Pakistani border. Terry, Rob's mother, died a few days after her son was flown home to undergo months of heroic surgeries.

Billy Paul's imaginary Swedish soccer team, courtesy of Big Red, was all he had left. It added some significance to his life.

"Can you imagine two farts like us lugging eighty pounds of gear over goat-dung mountain trails?" said Kelly.

Billy Paul cackled his response.

The drunk at the other end of the bar raised his empty shot glass. "God b-bless them grunts!"

Kelly was on empty too. "Where the hell did the years go, B-P?"

"Take it from me," his partner grimaced. "Once you turn fifty, time accelerates. It ain't no illusion, pal. Time moves faster. I guess it's the good Lord's way of reminding us we're short-timers."

"Speak for yourself," said Kelly, hailing another round.

"Oh, yeah? Well, you better grab one of them women you keep lyin' to and make yourself an honest life."

"My life's honest enough already, partner," he laughed.

"Hell, you don't even have a dog!"

Buster set down two more beers and tossed in a couple more bags of peanuts.

"Besides," said Kelly. "Women today are looking for short term re-lationships."

Billy Paul shot an accusing finger his way. "I'm talking long-term."

"What's that?"

"It's called marriage."

Most of Kelly's relationships wound up in bed and for about as long. Most of the others stopped seeing him for lack of interest; Homeland Security saw to that. Kelly grabbed his beer by the neck and took a long swig.

"Marriage s-sucks!" stuttered the drunk, knocking over his empty shot glass.

"I know one thing," said Kelly. "I don't want to wind up like that guy over there."

"Then get yourself an honest woman."

"How's that football team of yours coming along?" Kelly asked, changing the subject.

"Best ever," he said, a tired Cheshire grin creasing his small leathery face. "I programmed a dream team that's gonna take me all the way to the World Cup."

"What's wrong with football?"

"It is football, goofball! They call it soccer here. Football over there."

"If it makes you happy—"

"I know the whole thing's nothing more than a product of my imagination. But it plays like the real thing. I even get the team owner on the sideline telling me who to play and who I should take out."

"You're kidding."

"Big Red's as real as it gets, pal. It's hard to believe it's all up here," Billy Paul said tapping his forehead with a middle finger.

Kelly still couldn't wrap his head around the assignment. What did Homeland want with it anyway? Big Red had been around for almost four years. It was conceived and put together by an American company and sold on the commercial market worldwide. It didn't make sense. Product Division was nothing more than a tool in some government box against international bad guys trying tp blow up the world. Chapman's interest in a popular gaming system like DreamQwest kind of blurred the lines a bit.

Both called it a night a beer later.

*   *   *

"Another coffee, sir?" asked one of the hostesses in the sterile, nearly deserted airport lounge. It was 6 AM.

"I'm fine," Kelly winked, leaning back in a padded lounge chair, typical airport music playing softly overhead, interrupted occasionally with flight schedules.

He was now alone with his Ultra.

There was one new email. An incident report. Agency origin and document number indicated it was a 302. Why would Homeland send him a 302?

*   *   *

AT APPROXIMATELY 10:45 AM ON NOVEMBER 18th, 2025, THE DECEASED, MARCY AUBRY COLLINS, WHITE FEMALE, AGE 37, FEDERAL PROSECUTOR FOR THE STATE OF ILLINOIS, WAS FOUND DEAD IN AN UPRIGHT POSITION ON A LIVING ROOM COUCH IN HER CHICAGO LAKEFRONT CONDOMINIUM. THE DECEASED HAD REQUESTED A WEEK OFF ON THE 10th OF NOVEMBER AFTER INFORMING HER OFFICE SHE WANTED SOME TIME OFF. THE DECEASED NOTIFIED IN-HOUSE SECURITY ON THE 10th NOTIFYING CONDO SECURITY SHE WAS NOT TO BE DISTURBED.

THE ILLINOIS PROSECUTOR'S OFFICE IN CHICAGO GREW CONCERNED WHEN THE DECEASED FAILED TO RETURN TO WORK ON NOVEMBER 17th DESPITE SEVERAL ATTEMPTS TO REACH HER VIA PHONE AND EMAIL

CHICAGO POLICE RESPONDED WITH A 'CHECK ON THE WELL BEING'. FAILING A RESPONSE, AUTHORIZATION WAS GRANTED FOR FORCED ENTRY WHEREUPON THEY FOUND THE DECEASED SITTING ON A COUCH WEARING A BIG RED GAMING DEVICE.

MARCY COLLINS WAS PRONOUNCED BY MEDICAL PERSONNEL AT 10:45. AM ON THE 18TH.

FBI AND CRIME SCENE PERSONNEL ARRIVED AT APPROXIMATELY 12:20 PM THE SAME DAY. THE BODY WAS

SUBSEQUENTLY TRANSPORTED TO THE CHICAGO MED-
ICAL EXAMINERS OFFICE PENDING AN AUTOPSY.

IN-HOUSE CCTV FILM FOOTAGE REVEALED NO EV-
IDENCE OF CRIMINAL ENTRY. THERE WERE NO
REPORTS OF DISTURBANCES OR UNAUTHORIZED
PERSONS IN THE VICINITY BY IN-HOUSE SECURITY.
FORENSICS AND CRIME SCENE PERSONNEL FOUND
NO PRINTS OR EVIDENCE ASSOCIATED WITH CRIM-
INAL ENTRY.

Why a 302? It was what the F-B-I used. Kelly's assignment was nothing more than a property transfer. As far as he knew, the case was closed.

Or was it?

The email disappeared before he could save it.

CHAPTER TWO

Chicago's O'Hare was a frosty 22 degrees when his plane taxied to a stop. Forecasters predicted it would climb to the mid-thirties by noon. The wind coming off Lake Michigan told Kelly otherwise.

He already missed Seattle.

Kelly felt bad leaving Billy Paul by himself. The calendar was against him. The holiday season for most wouldn't actually begin until Thanksgiving.

An election had already come and gone and a new president had been elected. It was also hunting season for those whose careers were already on life-support; like holdovers from the previous administration. It also was no secret the in-coming president wanted a leaner and meaner Department of Homeland Security with little or no affinity toward Product Division that was eating up much of the federal budget along with its finite resources.

That there would be budget cuts was a given. Kelly could potentially lose his job in a new administration. Maybe that was the reason why Chapman was sticking his neck out on this one.

In any case, Kelly was expendable.

Would he be going back to being a Treasury agent? It was either that, or early retirement. Maybe invest what little money he had in DreamQwest?

The Virtual Reality craze with its ungainly V-R goggles had wetted America's appetite as a revolutionary new gaming experiences; although V-R goggles had been around for many years-—until DreamQwest entered the market with its Big Red.

The Big Red had created something entirely new beginning in 2024; a much more realistic and totally immersive experience that now threatened not only the entire V-R gaming industry, but the travel, entertainment, and leisure industries.

The Virtual-Reality people were now finding it harder and harder to turn a profit.

DreamQwest, in record time, had become the Amazon of the gaming world with its new, totally immersive gaming platform. Its only sin was that it had come up with a better mouse trap.

Big Red's overwhelming popularity, according to reviewers back in twenty-twenty-four, was that it allowed people to travel just about anywhere in the world, experience any adventure, from the comfort of a chair that was indistinguishable from reality.

As a result, the gaming, tourism, and film industry, were crying rape.

Airline and hotel chains, both domestic and foreign, all failed to reach their yearly profit goals due to Big Red's successes. Ticket sales across the board plunged as demand for the new gaming product was now world-wide in scope.

High-budget movie producers barely recouped production costs. Overall recreation stocks declined ten percent six months after Big Red hit the streets. All claimed DreamQwest had violated fair trade and monopoly laws.

Kelly thought it was all bullshit. He was no gamer. Never was. But he believed DreamQwest had the right to manufacture and sell any product so long as it didn't violate any laws, or hurt someone.

In this case it was Marcy Collins.

Kelly found a cab.

"The Green Tree."

All he knew on arrival was that the crime scene was on the twenty-first floor. Most of the elevators were already in use, or had people waiting in line. Only one came with a Chicago police officer holding a clipboard. Kelly recognized a crime scene when he saw one.

*   *   *

"Can I help you, sir?"

Kelly showed his I.D. The officer surrendered his clipboard.

"I see the F-B-I's still here," Kelly said, scribbling his name under Agent Alec Farris' signature.

"Yes, sir—he's been up there all morning."

The officer inserted a card. The elevator door hushed open.

Kelly noticed only three buttons: "P' for Penthouse. The other two were designated 'Lobby' and 'Garage' L and G.

"It's a twenty-one story building," said Kelly. "Usually there are a few floors in between."

"It's Ms. Collin's elevator, sir—or was."

The ascent was quick.

Kelly stepped out onto a plush green shag in the middle of an upscale condominium few public servants could afford.

The smell was something else. How could he forget the stench of death?

Body fluids and feces: The stink of death being directly proportionate to the number of days a body lay at rest during the process of decomposition. The central heat only made it worse.

The stench had tainted everything: walls, rugs, curtains, the very fabric of the high-end furniture that populated its spacious living room. The only way to improve it was getting rid of everything including the wallpaper.

"Cleaning people are scheduled tomorrow morning," came a voice from inside an open bedroom to his right. A dark suit in a heavy unbuttoned black overcoat appeared.

"Alec Farris. F-B-I." he said, extending his hand.

"Frank Kelly. Homeland Security."

"Sorry I didn't get a chance to call you. The Bureau wanted it dropped off at evidence custodian."

"I thought—?"

"They wanted it by the book. Eyes dotted. The total package. You know how that works."

Kelly knew exactly how that worked. He was still pissed.

"She was sitting on the couch when we found her," said Farris. "I just wanted to make sure we didn't miss anything."

Kelly's attention turned to the couch.

A brownish-black smudge stained one of its cushions. Fecal matter, possibly mixed with urine. A body's blood, like any fluid, sought its own level. In this case, it had settled below the level of Collins' dead heart manifested as a dark discoloration of the skin in the lower extremities from the waist down to her legs where the decomposing blood had settled.

"Autopsy showed she'd been dead approximately a week," said Farris, taking note of Kelly's interest. "Room temperature was set at eighty-six degrees."

"I can smell it."

"Some people like it hot," Farris smiled. "Nothing out of place. She kept it nice."

Kelly noticed the open curtains revealing the French doors leading out onto a brick-lined patio crowded with empty pots atop a four-foot wall.

"No need for curtains twenty-one stories above Lake Michigan," Farris observed.

"Something else looks interesting." Kelly pointed to the walls. "They're bare. No photos. No memorabilia. Nothing."

"We noticed it, too. We searched. Found nothing. Spotless. Cleanest scene I've ever seen. No plates, gum wrappers, newspapers, bag of chips, water bottles, tossed socks, shoes, the usual things you'd find from a person on vacation."

"What about the kitchen?" said Kelly.

"Collins had ready-to-eat meals in the freezer. Waste baskets were empty. Clothes in the dryer. That's it."

Farris grabbed a scrapbook off an end table and flipped it open.

Inside was an 8-by-12 color photograph of three women arm-in-arm. "The Collins woman." he said pointing to the one in the middle. "She hadn't changed much—the face, I mean."

"An American flag against a black curtain background," said Kelly. "Could be anywhere."

Farris flipped the photo, "August twenty-twenty." He slipped the photo back in the scrapbook and started flipping the pages. "Magazine clippings of young men in various stages of undress."

"For some people it's stamps," said Kelly.

"She's a player."

"Player?"

"Big Red. I take it you don't play,' said Farris. "Clippings and photos. It's what she used to set up her scenarios."

"I take it you do."

"Doesn't everybody?" Farris smiled. "I like cruises myself."

"The device goes for a thousand bucks a pop—no thanks."

Crime scenes were part of his D-N-A after all. It didn't make sense. How does someone die playing a game? A young prosecutor with a great career—or maybe not. The shame of it all was that a week from now she'd be forgotten. Nothing more than a statistic.

"What's this?" Kelly pointed out.

Farris pulled out the brochure from between the pages.

"Senator Dirk Crawford's presidential campaign brochure," said Kelly. "She was a supporter."

"He's going to be your next president," said Farris. "Look—I gotta go," he said walking Kelly to the elevator. "What exactly do you do at Homeland?" He punched the elevator to the garage twenty-two stops down.

"Electronic gadgets coming in from Asia. We check for subliminal messages directed at possible terrorist sleeper cells."

Farris wasn't impressed. "Sounds exciting."

The elevator hit bottom.

"Be careful," Farris cautioned, "Stay away from the main lobby. Reporters like to beat a dead horse until it shits—if you know what I mean."

The door hushed open. In front of Kelly was a midnight blue BMW sitting by itself in a garage made for two.

"Nice wheels," said Kelly. "Private penthouse. Personal elevator. I didn't know federal prosecutors earned that much."

Farris didn't respond. He used the same card to open a side door leading out into general parking.

"An upscale prison," said Farris, pointing up at the CCTV cameras. He seemed in a hurry. "I'd give you a lift, but I have court in half an hour."

No—go ahead. I have to get moving myself."

Kelly found an escalator going up to the lobby.

A middle-aged man in a pin-stripe suit and bow-tie met him as he stepped off.

They needed no introduction.

Kelly had introduced himself to the in-house man in charge of security when he arrived to let him know he was there on official business. More a professional courtesy. The security manager, Richard Head, like some security managers, knew nothing about security.

"A real mess," Head complained. "Never know what kind of clientele you're going to get," he said shaking his head.

Kelly turned on him. "Aside from the fact one of your residents died, I don't think it'll take management long to start renting it out again."

It was as if Kelly had insulted his mother. "We don't rent," Head replied indignantly.

"If you don't mind me asking, how much do they go for?"

"If you're looking to buy," Head smirked, "I'm afraid it may be above your paygrade, Agent Kelly."

"I asked you a simple question—Dick."

Head backed off and cleared his throat. "We, uh, start at five hundred thousand. Miss Collins' penthouse goes for one point three mill."

Not on a federal prosecutor's salary, he thought. A rich uncle? Not Uncle Sam for sure. The federal government would have spotted any discrepancy. Background checks and financial statements were a yearly norm. Every employee, including the politicians, had to submit one.

"See ya later, Dick."

Head caught him before he got far.

"The news people pulled up about an hour ago. Main entrance. Maybe you could put in a few good words—"

Kelly had already spotted the van with its satellite dish and camera crew out on the sidewalk through the lobby's smoked-glass façade.

"You have a side entrance?"

"Loading dock down the hallway to your right."

The last thing Kelly wanted was to see himself on the six o'clock news. He found a cab on a trash strewn side street half a block away.

"Where to, Bud?"

Kelly's Ultra sounded as he hopped in.

"This is evidence custodian Baily. We're releasing an item to your custody as per our conversation with Agent Alec Farris. It's awaiting pickup on Michigan."

Farris, it seemed, was as much in a hurry to get rid of Big Red as Kelly was to get back to Seattle; back to keeping the bad guys from using children's toys from blowing up the world.

"Storm's coming," the cabby warned. "Where to?"

Kelly still couldn't rap his head around the case. Was Chapman alone in this, or getting pressured from someone upstream? Nothing was right about any of it. And where did the Collins' woman get the money to afford a penthouse worth over a million? It had been said that a rich person couldn't get into heaven; but there was no law that said a rich person couldn't work for the government. If that was the case, Kelly was in the wrong business.

The assignment was beginning to stink worse than a dog fart.

In his profession there was an unwritten rule that said if one had more questions than answers, then one had to stop asking questions and start turning over some rocks.

The opposite was also true: Never turn over a rock if you're afraid of what you'll find.

Kelly would find out soon enough.

"The meter's running," the cabby complained.

"Police Administration Building."

"South Michigan—sure."

CHAPTER THREE

The evidence room was no different from any other. It came with a counter and plexiglass shield. The kind found in banks, though Kelly couldn't remember the last time an evidence room was held up at gunpoint in the basement of police headquarters.

Behind it was a civil service employee trying to look busy.

"Whataya got?" the clerk said, irritably, snatching the property receipt out of Kelly's hand. Like Santa Claus, he checked it twice.

"You Agent Farris?"

Kelly showed him his I.D. "Frank Kelly. Homeland Security. You Bailey?"

"No. That was a recording you got."

"It's Kelly. Frank Kelly."

"Yeah. Okay. I see it now," said the clerk, looking up. "Frank Kelly. Homeland Security. Product Division. Never heard of it."

Kelly smiled. "That's good."

"How'd you wind up with a tit job like that?"

"Since we're hearing confessions, you go first."

The clerk looked at him with hostile indifference then turned and walked back into a labyrinth of metal shelving, pulling out a plastic bin.

"I got one of these gizmos for my grandson last Christmas. Cost me a bundle. The game alone—"

"Look, I got a cab waiting upstairs."

The clerk took out what looked like an apple-red pilot's helmet without a visor and set it down on the counter.

"Don't hurry back," said the clerk.

Chicago, like most urban centers, had long ago outgrown its highways. They were moving from one traffic light to another.

"This is going to take a while," said the cabby. "Looks like everybody left work early. They say Wisconsin got two feet."

Kelly was in no hurry. His flight to Washington wasn't set to leave until tomorrow morning. It was now going on two-thirty according to the cab's dashboard. He had time to kill. Maybe a shower, grab a bite to eat, unwind a bit before turning in.

"You know, my twelve-year-old asked me for one of those the other day," the cabby said, his eyes looking down at him from the rearview mirror. "I take it you're a gamer."

"It's for an acquaintance."

"Sure," the cabby laughed, until something caught his attention in the mirror. "You're being followed."

"How can you tell?" said Kelly, taking what he said as a joke.

"Believe me, I can tell. My creditors are a bit more direct. "

Kelly glanced into the driver's side mirror. A black Suburban. It wasn't the FBI. US Marshals maybe. The bureau didn't use them for tailing—too obvious. But a lot of people drove black Suburbans, including himself.

"I haven't been in Chicago long enough to make enemies," said Kelly.

The cabby smiled back at him from his mirror.

"Just get me to a hotel near the airport," said Kelly.

*　　　*　　　*

They were all full.

Kelly found one of O'Hare's security doors and punched in his government code allowing him access to a well-lit corridor populated by airport supervisors and managers, airport maintenance, government officials of every stripe like the F-B-I, or Customs and other credentialed employees whose job it was to get to where they wanted to go quickly without having to stand in line at security kiosks. There was more traffic than usual. Kelly found out why when he found the terminal he wanted and exited.

*   *   *

It was standing room only. That meant cancelled flights. The arrival and departure monitors resembled a stock market crash. Delayed. Delayed. Delayed…

One person stood out from the crowd: a man in uniform holding a sign with Kelly's name on it in bold black letters with captain's sleeves, crushed hat, and silver wings. The only thing missing on his hat was a propeller. He was checking his Ultra when Kelly confronted him.

The uniform turned his Ultra around showing a recent government file photo of Kelly in full color.

"Getting hard up for passengers?" Kelly asked him.

"Captain Alex Milford. Five Star Executive," the man replied, tipping his crushed hat with a smile. "I'm your pilot."

Kelly flipped out his badge. "Says who?"

Milford handed over his Ultra. "Mister Atwater would like to speak to you, sir."

"I see you are in possession of one of my Big Reds," replied a young, educated voice.

"Your man here's in possession of a government-issued Ultra."

"We seem to be at an impasse, Agent Kelly. Allow me to introduce myself. My name is Jason Atwater. C-E-O of DreamQwest Corporation. The manufacturer of that government-issued Ultra." The voice deepened. *"Did you read the 302 I sent you?"*

"That was you?"

"I have my share of enemies, Agent Kelly. They would like nothing better than to see me selling pencils in Times Square."

"That's not my problem, pal."

"I'm sure you must have some questions of your own. Like why Homeland wants that Big Red you're carrying? The F-B-I facility at Quantico would have been the best and most logical choice, not Homeland."

"What're you getting at?"

"Why are you involved at all? What does the Deputy Secretary of Homeland Security want with this particular Big Red? Neither your facility in Seattle, nor Washington have the technology to determine what caused Ms. Collins' death."

Kelly could think of no credible reason to counter his argument. He'd asked himself that same question. Why hadn't the F-B-I taken possession of the device? It was their case after all. They had the equipment. Chapman knew as much about the device as he did.

"Who better than the manufacturer, Agent Kelly?"

"You want the device."

"Simply borrow it—"

"Sorry, but this big boy stays with me."

"I admire your integrity. If you wish you may come along as my guest. I can have you in Washington no later than tomorrow afternoon with no one the wiser. No expense will be spared. I guarantee you no one will know."

"We better get going," said the pilot. "Weather's getting ugly."

The luxury executive jet was a twelve-seater. Kelly was out-numbered by three young attendants with million-dollar smiles along with resumes that would make a human resources manager salivate. All were multilingual, well-versed in the stock market, and capable of prolonged conversations virtually on any topic, current or otherwise.

By the time the flight ended at Kalamazoo-Battle Creek International in Michigan, he had had a manicure, two beers, and a detailed summary and analysis on post-Roman European history.

*   *   *

The plane taxied to a stop in a remote, private service area within a barbed-wire enclosure surrounded by a forest of leafless trees and a grey menacing sky.

"This way, sir," said the pilot, exiting the plane as the folding steps lowered to meet the ground. Kelly followed. He handed Kelly a set of keys.

"Suzy will take you the rest of the way, sir."

"Who's Suzy?"

The pilot pointed to a small nondescript compact parked off to one side of the tarmac. It had Ohio plates, missing a hubcap, and in need of a paint job.

"She'll take you the rest of the way, Mr. Kelly."

"That the best you can do?"

"We're not in the rental business, sir."

Kelly set the Big Red on the back seat along with his backpack. By the time he got in and turned the key, the pilot and attendants were gone.

"Remain in this lane for the next three miles," came a pleasant voice over the dashboard.

The dark, slate-grey sky ahead warned of snow. His thoughts turned to Billy Paul back in beautiful forty-eight-degree Seattle.

"Make a right turn at the next exit. Stay in your right lane for the next one and a half miles. Then turn left."

Kelly almost missed the sign: ATWATER BLVD.

"You have to be kidding."

"I didn't get hat," said Suzy.

Not many people had their own four-lane highway. Then again, an enterprise like DreamQwest could do just about anything it wanted.

"Exit now!"

"Okay, okay."

A frozen lake lay up a ways off to his right. Isolated pockets of verdant pines, and something else off in the grey distance fast approaching over a rolling landscape of frozen tundra. The complex resembled a scene out of the Wizard of Oz.

"You have arrived," Suzy announced, giving him a brief virtual tour of the campus.

DreamQwest Corporation sat on 800 acres of pristine parkland in Calhoun County, Michigan. It wasn't Seattle. Then again it occurred to Kelly that maybe it was supposed to look like this in mid- November in Michigan.

Kelly couldn't get over how massive it was.

Four huge cylindrical-shaped chrome towers, each crowned by a pyramid-like structure against a dark electric sky occupied all four corners of the complex. To its right was a Romanesque courtyard guarded by armless granite statues in mute testimony to the company's good fortune. Wally World for gamers, he thought.

"I'm-off-to-see-the-Wizard—-," Kelly hummed, though he didn't get the chance to finish it.

Suzy slowed as it approached a cascade of marble steps leading up to a shallow cobalt blue wall protecting the complex. It had two massive doors, almost vault-like, the DreamQwest logo blazing red in bold Gothic letters above them.

"You accept tips?" he asked Suzy.

"No payment is required, Mr. Kelly. I wish you a productive stay."

A huge uniformed guard, his right hand gripping a loaded holster, descending the steps three at a time.

"I-D, please," the guard ordered. Kelly obliged. "Thank you, sir. Mr. Atwater is expecting you."

"The device stays with me," said Kelly, grabbing the Big Red from the back seat.

"Yes, sir." The big guard started back up the steps. "Follow me, sir."

"I'm armed."

"So are we, sir."

The guard stood a good foot taller. An easy three hundred pounds in a dark blue jacket matching his deep blue uniform, his two massive arms on a barreled chest with a face as wide as his thick neck.

"You ever play football?" Kelly asked on his way up the steps.

"No, sir."

The lobby was grandiose with walls covered in abstract art. He'd seen better in subway tunnels.

"This way, sir!" the guard cautioned, re-directing him away from a bank of metal detectors. "Don't want to trip any alarms," he said. "You've already been cleared, sir."

Kelly noticed CCTV cameras whirring overhead along with some other gadgets he had no idea what they did for a living.

They emerged into a vast, open courtyard.

The big man climbed into one of a dozen covered shuttles. "Come aboard, sir." he said, waving Kelly to join him.

"Does all this belong to DreamQwest?"

"All eight hundred acres, sir."

The sky was growing darker.

"It's going to snow," said Kelly. "You're going to need snow tires by tonight."

"The concourse is porous, sir. And heated. The runoff drains out into the fountain area."

"Sweden has a similar system."

"You been there, sir?"

"No. National Geographic."

"Tower One's just up ahead, sir.".

From what Kelly could see there were three just like it off in the not so far distance, like points on a compass.

The shuttle stopped in front of an ornate entrance guarded by art deco gargoyles seemingly supporting it on folded dragon wings.

"The penthouse is on the twenty-first floor," the guard explained, turning off the shuttle.

"The view must be great from the top," said Kelly.

"There are no windows, sir."

It started snowing as they entered.

The guard inserted a card into a slot. "Penthouse."

There were others: Human Resources along with five other floors in numerical order marked Living Quarters: 2 thru 12, and Executive Suites: 14 thru 20.

A few seconds later the doors opened revealing a brightly lit corridor. At the other end a pair of massive bronze metal doors opened slowly to Handel's Messiah.

"I'll be here when you come out, sir."

The executive suite was spartan as compared to most.

"Welcome, Agent Kelly," greeted a frail young man sitting behind a massive ebony desk dressed in a black suit and black turtleneck sweater.

Kelly wanted to be sure. "Atwater?"

"Yes. In the flesh, I'm afraid."

The grey painted walls were covered with what appeared to be large comic book posters with DreamQwest logos sequenced by title and year mounted on polished brass plaques: Pro Football; Pro Soccer 2026; Baseball and American Hockey 2027; Safari; Survival; Triassic Hunt; Cruise Line 2028; World Travel and Pro Golf.

The last was Garden of Eden.

"Please." Atwater's smile seemed to relax. "Be seated, Agent Kelly."

The huge ebony chrome metaled desk mimicked the building's external architecture. A chrome clock with a stainless-steel ball in perpetual motion enclosed in a glass case at one end. A Quantum laptop sat at desk center in ebony plastic.

A rich kid in an expensive sandbox, Kelly thought.

"You must be tired, Agent Kelly."

Kelly approached the desk and set the Big Red down on the desk before seating himself in one of two black leather armchairs. Plush and deep, gently vibrating, heated to body temperature. Kelly noticed it came with a built-in Ultra phone and other buttons he couldn't quite make out what they did for a living.

"Would you mind if I call you Frank?"

"It's your quarter—Jason."

Atwater reached across the desk, touching Big Red tenderly with the soft tips of his delicate fingers.

"I trust your trip was a pleasant one."

"Better than most airlines."

"And my girls?"

"Very attentive."

Atwater caressed the Big Red like a kid welcoming home a long-lost pet. "I hire the absolute best and brightest. Harvard and M-I-T. Beauty is nothing without brains."

Kelly glanced at his watch. "I'm here. Now what?"

"Have you tried any of our games, Frank?"

"I'm not a gamer."

"They are quite the experience. You should try a few."

"I don't believe Marcy Collins would agree with you on that."

"Ahh, yes. Most unfortunate." Jason Atwater poured the remains of a carafe of coffee into a black porcelain mug.

There was something about Atwater's head that caught Kelly's attention. It wasn't symmetrical. The right side looked proportionally different from the left—or maybe it was the way he combed his hair that morning.

Atwater seemed unsure of what he wanted to say next.

"I truly thank you for accepting my offer."

"You understand that device on your desk is government property."

"And it will remain so, Frank. I guarantee it."

"You also understand I was never here."

"I have temporarily altered your Ultra's locator for just such a possibility. From what my meteorologists tell me the storm is rather significant. Record snowfall. Flights will be stacked up for at least the next twelve hours. Your Ultra will alert whomever is calling that you are still at O'Hare waiting for the weather to clear. We have a good forty hours before anyone pushes the panic button."

"I gave you twenty four."

"Trust me, Frank. No one will know you were here."

"Okay. What are you planning to do with that?"

"A thorough inspection, of course. What happened in Chicago must not occur again."

"What do you call thorough?"

"All Big Red's have a data disc. Hopefully, it will tell us what happened the day Marcy Collins's died. You will be present during the screening of course. I will see to it you and Big Red reach Washington as promised."

"Original condition."

"You have my word." Atwater glanced down at his watch. "Hungry?"

The doors swung open ushering in a slim, attractive woman with short copper-colored hair with large copper earrings dressed in tight baby-blue mini- shorts with a translucent white blouse that revealed ample cleavage. The plush white shag rug silencing her well-heeled footfalls. She placed a large white porcelain tray on the desk, smiled mechanically, and left.

Atwater followed her out with his eyes.

"Thank you, Nicole."

The offerings were two glasses of milk and a dozen chocolate donut holes. Kelly passed on both.

"Great artwork."

"Excuse me?"

"The posters," said Kelly. "On your walls."

Atwater giggled like a five-year-old. "They represent the games we offer to our customers—or so they say."

"Wait a minute." Kelly leaned forward "Are you saying you never played?"

"To be quite honest, I prefer the here and now." Atwater's apology was weak. "I have everything I want and need right here."

The Quantum on his desk chimed.

"Ah, the autopsy report. Would you like to see it, Frank?"

"That's not for public consumption—"

Atwater cracked a Cheshire grin. "I have my sources."

"You should be working for the government, Jason."

"I am afraid that would be quite impossible. I am far too organized. The government wastes so much money on the wrong things. It needs to develop a better understanding of what is in the national interest."

"Politics is in the national interest," said Kelly.

"You are so right. Maybe I should develop a game strictly for politicians on how to run a country. Something on the order of Sim City."

"How old are you, Jason?"

Atwater hesitated. "Does it matter?"

Kelly never believed in preordained destiny; an oxymoron in any case. A god with a sense of humor maybe. The Atwater's of the world were no doubt ambitious types, driven by something no ordinary person possessed; born with an uncanny talent for success that eluded most people. History wasn't exactly loaded with human prodigies.

Blessings, as well as the curses in life, are merely two sides of the same coin for people like Jason Atwater.

For most everyone else success was a series of hits and misses, and unemployment checks.

Atwater's mood suddenly turned darkly. He popped another donut hole, momentarily raising his spirits.

"Dr. Nigel Atwater was my grandfather," Atwater confessed. "He was a physics professor at Berkley for many years. You may have heard of one of his books. The author of Nectar of the Gods."

Who hadn't?

Kelly settled back in the comfort of his warm and gently vibrating chair. As a former cop, he had learned the importance of listening. It was amazing how many people self-incriminated simply by talking too much.

So far Jason Atwater had stuck to the script.

It was now a matter of trust.

The book was one of those pseudo-spirituality books popular with the young college crowd. The girl Kelly was seeing on campus at the time talked incessantly about weird, paranormal things, as if normal wasn't spooky enough. She had quoted extensively from passages in the book whenever Kelly went to her room feigning interest in the book only long enough to collect his reward. Most of the time not.

"Grandfather went broke developing the theory that led to Big Red's later success. It was my father, Nathaniel Atwater, who financed the project." Jason Atwater spoke with a quiet, yet disturbed dignity. "He was a stockbroker. Well-known in investment circles. He made a lot of money doing the wrong things. I'm surprised he didn't go to jail. Barnard Collins was my father's attorney. The executor of his estate."

It didn't sink in at first. "Collins—?"

"Marcy Collins' father—yes." Jason Atwater leaned back in his chair taking his mug of coffee with him. "Marcy graduated college while I was still in high school. She was a sister I never had."

"So, you have a dog in this fight."

"Let us say I am very interested—yes." Atwater picked up the autopsy report and read it aloud:

"Asphyxiation due to pulmonary valve stenosis was at first suspected but eliminated as a factor, subsequently attributed to the decomposition process. Blood work was inconclusive. No hallucinogenic drugs or controlled substances found other than the F-D-A approved additive Two-Seven-Five."

"So how did she die?"

"Further examination revealed no arterial atheroma associated with sudden adult death syndrome. She was not a smoker. No traumas indicated. The deceased enjoyed exceptional health." Atwater turned to Kelly. "She should not have died."

Jason Atwater leaned forward and pointed to a small bulbous rubber valve on Big Red's inflatable collar.

"During game-play the collar automatically inflates. The collar is designed to keep out light and external noise during game play. It also controls Big Red's environmental integrity, including oxygen and temperature control."

"She was hermetically sealed."

"Yes," said Atwater, glancing at his watch.

"But what if the collar malfunctioned and...?"

"If for any reason the system fails, the user presses this rubber valve. It purges air pressure thus deflating the collar allowing the user to exit Big Red. If this fails, you simply close your eyes for fifteen seconds. The collar then deflates automatically."

"According to the investigators they easily removed the Big Red."

"Precisely why I wanted the Big Red. Who better to find out what happened that night than the manufacturer?"

The doors opened again. An attractive woman in her early thirties strode briskly into the office. Unlike Nicole, she was conservatively dressed in a dark wool business suit. The briefcase gave away her profession.

Atwater got up and rounded the desk.

"If you will excuse me, Frank, I am late for a meeting. Brenda Farrell, my corporate attorney, will further assist you," he said, snatching a black corduroy coat from a wall rack on his way out. "Be nice to him, Brenda."

Brenda Farrell set her briefcase down on the desk, pulling out some paperwork, and slapped them down in front of him.

"Sign them," she said, dropping a pen on the desk to make sure he did.

"What's this?"

"A non-disclosure agreement. It means anything you see or hear remains here."

"Can't do that."

"Standard procedure—Kelly is it?"

"If I sign that, it means I was here."

"Aren't you?"

"Look, Counselor—"

"It's standard procedure," she said, taking a seat behind the desk.

"The solution's simple." Kelly got up. "I'll just take that giant cherry and be on my way."

"Sit down," she said quietly.

"Are you always this angry?"

"I'm here to protect the interests of DreamQwest Corporation."

"And mine, I hope. If they find out—"

"Your name is Frank Kelly. You are presently employed as a federal agent assigned to Homeland Security for the past two years and eight months. Before that you were a Treasury agent, and before that a cop—"

"I don't have to be here, Counselor."

"So what exactly do you do for Homeland?"

"You tell me."

"Correct me if I'm wrong. Product Division. Created in twenty twenty-four. Part of a national security program designed to thwart terrorist organizations from smuggling compromised electronic products into the United States."

Kelly leaned back in his chair. "We deal in imported products. Not domestic."

"So you shouldn't object to signing this agreement."

Like any lawyer, Brenda Farrell dealt only in the cold facts with a natural predatory instinct that helped her win cases. Collins meant nothing to her. She was merely a statistic. Until that morning when Collins awoke thinking what adventure lie in store not yet knowing she was about to die playing a popular virtual reality game like millions of others that cold November morning in the warmth and comfort of her own living room.

Kelly remembered something that was in the autopsy report.

"What's a Two-Seven-Five?"

Brenda Farrell was caught off guard for a moment.

"It's an enhancer," she said defensively. "A protein developed from Mediterranean squid glands. It helps with the gaming experience. Fully approved by food and drug. A requirement, actually."

"Squid glands."

"Totally safe. Developed right here in our labs."

"So, it's a drug."

"Depends what you mean by drugs. Coffee's a drug." said Farrell. Approved by the FDA. It comes in three chewable flavors: vanilla, strawberry, and mint. It causes no flashbacks or psychological dependency."

"What about booze?"

"Drinking an alcoholic beverage in excess will interfere with the gaming experience causing at most a hangover. In any case there is nothing in the report indicating she had anything to drink."

"Have you tried it?"

"I'm a gamer. Yes. Big Red enhances what the brain sees, hears, smells, and feels. I would say it's a rather enjoyable experience, and wonderfully entertaining as well as being perfectly safe."

"Safe."

"I know what you're doing," she said, noticing the autopsy report Atwater had left on the desk. She grabbed it and stuffed it into her briefcase.

"You always this miserable?"

Brenda Farrell stood up, leaving the unsigned non-disclosure document on the desk. "Nine o'clock tomorrow," she said, rising to her feet. "A procedure will take place in Tower Two. Third floor. Nine o'clock. Don't be late."

"What's going to happen in Tower Two?"

"Nine o'clock."

"Okay. Nine o'clock," he said, grabbing Big Red as he got up.

"I nearly forgot," she said, handing Kelly a key card. "The Radnor is a DreamQwest property. Suzy knows where it is. Have a nice evening, Agent Kelly."

She didn't mean it.

CHAPTER FOUR

The Radnor Lakeside, it's fake turn-of-the-century exterior
barely visible through a windless snowfall. The lake, if there ever was
one, lay froze, and now covered in snow. Except for two cars parked on
the side of the hotel, it was empty.

"You have arrived," Suzy announced.

"I think so," he told her.

"Have a nice evening, sir."

Kelly made his way inside.

All he really needed was a shower. What little clothes he brought
with him was stuffed into backpack consisting of two pairs of black
flannel pants, one flannel shirt, two heavy sweaters, one white, one
brown, three pairs of socks and three changes of underwear, guaran-
tying most would be wrinkled beyond recognition in the morning.

The gilded lobby had more than its share of fine-art paintings
hung on silk walls; polished brass light fixtures adorned in sparkling
crystal, and a heavy oriental rug that silenced his every footfall.

DreamQwest had spared no expense, it seemed.

The lobby, of course, was empty except for a man in a tuxedo behind
a check-in desk who seemed not to know anyone was coming in ad-
vance.

"Any room on the second floor, Mr. Kelly. Dining room is closed.
Lounge is open. Down the hallway to your right. Have a nice evening,
sir."

Barring any surprises, he would be on his way to D.C. by noon tomorrow. Showered and shaved and a change of clothes an hour later,

he secured the Big Red on a back shelf in a mostly empty closet before heading down to the lounge.

Its theme was a turn-of-the-century gaslight parlor complete with a huge oil painting of a pleasantly smiling naked lady overlooking a Victorian bar matching the lounge's Victorian decor. A huge TV on the wall above the nude made him feel more at home.

"Whataya have?" the bartender asked, dressed like a Mississippi gambler, a toothpick dangling off his lip, trying hard not to notice him.

"I'll have tortilla chips with Jalapeno and cheese dip and a Sam Adams," said Kelly. His first meal since a breakfast bar that morning.

"No tortilla chips or Jalapeno," replied the bartender.

"Bean soup and a roll?"

"No bean soup." The bartender looked at him hard. "We have spinach with crotons."

"Who the hell eats spinach with crotons?"

"That's what we got," the bartender shrugged.

"What about a roast beef sandwich with horse radish?"

The bartender set down a tall glass of Sam Adams. "No horse radish."

"I noticed business is booming," said Kelly, sarcastically.

"Don't get many guests this time of year."

"What about potato chips and cheddar dip?"

The bartender slowly walked to the opposite end of the bar and returned with a bag of potato chips. "No dip," he said, clicking on the TV.

A panel of experts filled the huge TV screen discussing crime statistics.

"How 'bout that?" the Bartender said cracking a smile, the toothpick bouncing off his lip. "Sex crimes down for the second straight year."

"So they say," said Kelly, still working on his beer.

"Big Red's puttin' the damn perverts out of business."

"They're still in business," Kelly corrected him.

"How do you figure, Mister?"

"They're just using Big Red to do it."

"If you don't mind me askin' Mister, how'd you find this place? We don't get many—"

"Wiseguys?" Kelly took another swig of beer. "I'm Jason Atwater's guest." The bartender caught his toothpick before it hit the counter.

"Hey, Stevie," he shouted to someone in back. "Whip up a basket of tortilla chips with plenty of Jalapeño. Make it quick. Don't care how you do it!" The bartender shook his head in repentance.

"You actually seen 'em?"

"Who?"

"Atwater."

"Spoke to him about an hour ago."

"Nobody here's ever seen 'em," the bartender whispered hoarsely, his eyes scared open. "We call him Dracula—you know, the vampire."

"You mean the guy who signs your paychecks every week?"

The bartender backed off. "Hockey game's on, Mister. Detroit at Montreal."

"I'll have another beer."

"It's on the house."

There was no hockey game.

Instead, Kelly found himself staring up at the face of the Attorney General of the United States standing at a podium surrounded by half a dozen suits.

"What happened to the game?" the bartender protested.

"At approximately one forty-five this afternoon, Eleanor Chapman, wife of Deputy Secretary of Homeland Security, Peter J. Chapman, accompanied by her attorney, informed this office under oath that her husband, Peter J. Chapman, was having an affair with Illinois federal prosecutor Marcy Collins who, on the nineteenth of this month, was found dead in her Chicago Lakeside residence."

Kelly coughed up his beer.

"You okay, Mister?"

"As attorney general of the United States, I have decided to reopen the Marcy Collins case based on the credible testimony of Mrs. Chapman."

The attorney general babbled on, leaving Kelly to absorb the full impact of what he had heard.

And the possible impact it would have on his career.

*   *   *

Brenda Farrell had nearly given up when Kelly sauntered into the lobby nursing a coffee with a Big Red tucked under one arm.

"Have a bad night?" she said, bouncing a finger off her watch. It was past nine.

"I take it you guys didn't watch the evening news," he said, brushing the snow off the Big Red.

"I don't want to be late," she said, jumping into one of a line of shuttles in the lobby.

"Tower Two?"

"The lab where we develop Big Red."

It had been snowing most of the night. Suzy didn't do all that bad considering it was a piece of junk. Maybe that was it. Who'd want to steal it?

The concourse of course was wet, the snow melting on impact and drained off like the guard said.

"Tower One is administration and human resources," she explained. "Two is science; Tower Three is medical, and Four security and engineering. Altogether over two thousand employees, and families."

Kelly barely strapped in when Farrell throttled it, passing the murals in the lobby on her way across the open concourse.

"Who designed all this? Marvel Comics?"

"Jason Atwater is an eccentric," she admitted with soft reverence. ""I take it you're not a fan."

Farrell accelerated across the multi-acre concourse.

"Jason's already here," she said pulling next to a shuttle in one of the executive parking slots.

"Dump your coffee over there," she said, pointing to a blue box. "We're going to pathology."

"Pathology?" Kelly followed Farrell into its small lobby. "Big Red isn't organic. It's a toy," he said. She opened the elevator with her card.

"Level three," she said. The ride was short. "Jason believes they are one and the same."

"Why do you encourage him?"

"Who says he's wrong?"

Johann Sebastian Bach's Mass in B minor welcomed them as the elevator came to a smooth stop, opening to a brightly lit corridor with a heavy plexiglass wall at its near end.

A huddle of six men dressed in white protective gear were visible on the other side. It resembled more a surgical suite.

"Good morning, gentlemen," Farrell greeted via an intercom fixed to the wall. "Is it safe?"

A short, chunky, middle-aged man wearing a pair of Ben Franklin glasses quickly approached them from the other side and punched in a code.

A section of the wall opened.

The air was cold.

"Brenda. How nice to see you again. Jason told me you were coming."

"Where is he? I saw his shuttle—"

"I believe he's in production. He should be here shortly."

Kelly recognized some of the equipment. Most arrayed on stainless-steel tables. He had no clue what they did for a living.

The computers, of course, were Quantum.

All he ever needed in Seattle was a bar code reader and laptop.

"And who do we have the honor?" said Ben, looking up at Kelly.

"Frank Kelly. I'm one of Jason's friends," he said, feeling a quick, painful jab in the back from one of Farrell's fingers.

"Ben Nettlebaum," the little man replied, his eyes distorted behind his thick glasses. He seemed more interested in the Big Red. "I am director of research and development. Very pleased to meet you."

"Set down over there," said Farrell, pointing to one of the tables.

Kelly felt like the pied piper as they followed him to a stainless-steel table. It was quickly surrounded.

"Would you like me to explain the protocol?" said Ben, turning to face Kelly.

"Mr. Kelly can't stay long, Ben," Farrell explained. "We need to get started."

The lab wall opened again as Atwater stumbled in, clearly out of breath. "Have you started?"

"We were in the process," said Ben, keying in a series of commands on the Quantum. "We are a go, sir."

"How soon?"

"We need to transfer Ms. Collins H-V-D disc from her Big Red to our Quantum and synchronize the data. I would say an hour at most," Nettlebaum said, opening a small compartment on Big Red's inside collar, removing a two-inch gold-plated disk the size of a large coin.

Jason Atwater pulled Farrell aside. "Something's come up," he whispered.

"Yes, I know. The news. We don't have a lot of time before—-."

"Look," Atwater said quietly. "Why don't you take him to lunch while we download Collins' files."

"I'd rather get hit by a bus."

"It is not a request, Brenda."

*   *   *

There was the heavy scent of potato bread in the air when Kelly eased out of Farrell's blue Mercedes.

The Pirogi Restaurant had that East European façade about it.

"Looks pricey?" said Kelly, nearly losing his balance on the ice-encrusted curb. Farrell kicked her boots before going in.

"What are you worried about? It's on the house. Compliments of DreamQwest Corporation."

"Look," he said. "I could've gone to the Radnor—"

"You can tell your little friends you ate at the Pirogi. Okay?"

Kelly grabbed hold of her arm. "Hey—lighten up, lady. People are going to think I'm your husband."

"Get your hands off me," she snapped, reclaiming her arm, peeling out of her three-quarter fleece-lined coat as she entered, revealing a blue-sequin turtleneck sweater high-lighting an already statuesque figure.

Kelly noticed, of course.

"Don't be surprised if they ask where you parked your motorcycle," she said.

Kelly removed his black leather jacket. A cloakroom attendant came by and took their garments.

"Hello, Miss Farrell," greeted a gentle grey-haired lady in a pink apron with matching cheeks. She smelled of cooking. Her attention turned to Kelly. "And who is this good-looking young man?"

"Frank Kelly," he said, introducing himself.

"I'm Anna. Welcome to the Pirogi. We are pleased to have you."

Farrell made her way to a window table.

"Over there' would be better," Kelly said, redirecting her to a table near the kitchen doors.

"You must be hungry," she said.

"No one can hear what we say over there," he confided. Kelly looked over the menu as he settled into his chair. It wasn't cheap.

A waitress set down two glasses of water.

"I'll have the special," said Farrell without looking at the menu. "The Kielbasa and house salad."

"Vodka Martini?"

Farrell nodded her approval. "Don't forget the olives."

"And you, sir?"

"I'll take the Golumkies, no salad, and a Sam Adams. No olives."

The waitress smiled courteously and left.

"You don't make friends easily, do you?" said Farrell in a low whisper.

"That's why they don't let me out much," he laughed.

"I can believe that."

"I get the feeling you come here a lot."

"Often," said Farrell, her eyes less threatening. "Let's get this straight. I'm not comfortable with this arrangement. I still think the whole thing is a bad idea."

"You mean me."

The waitress returned a few minutes later with a Vodka Martini and a tall glass of Sam Adams.

"I was on my way to Washington when Jason called. I had some questions of my own about the Collins case."

"You were there?"

"Briefly. They had already taken her away when I got there."

Farrell stirred the Martini with her finger. "What was she to you?"

"The F-B-I was handling the case. Most of the evidence and forensic work was already done. All I did was pick up the Big Red."

"According to the FBI she was still wearing a Big Red when they found her," she said. "Nothing out of place. They never really determined cause of death."

"Jason read the full autopsy report. She was in apparent good health."

"What bothers me is why Homeland wants it?" she said, fishing an olive out of her glass.

"Not my paygrade."

"Blind obedience—right?"

"Look, lady. I could lose my job. If they find out I'm sitting here in a restaurant talking to a DreamQwest attorney while they take apart the very thing I was sent to—"

"What?"

"Look. I know less about this than anyone."

"By the end of the day what do you get out of it? A pat on the head?"

"Look. I'm risking twenty years in federal prison just talking to you, lady."

Brenda Farrell took another sip of her martini and fished out another olive.

"Forgive me for being overly curious," she said. "The F-B-I already dropped the case. Seriously, what does Homeland want with Big Red?"

"Your boss asked me that same question. I don't know—or care."

Farrell looked at him sideways. "What exactly do you do at Homeland?"

"There's two of us. We take random samples of imported toys and electronics from port of entry in Seattle, and determine whether they've been compromised."

"Toys," she said coyly, trying not to laugh. "I think you're putting me on."

"The concept started in Germany. Intelligence sources in the German Republic had intercepted intelligence that terrorists were trying to Import toys and other electronic devices using encrypted commands and codes for terrorist sleeper cells in Europe."

"Toys," Farrell repeated.

"You think it's funny? During the eighties, the Soviet Army in Afghanistan rigged children's toys with explosives. They left them in roadways near Afghan villages. They hoped the children would pick 'em up, take 'em back to their villages and go boom. They thought it would shorten the war."

"Did you ever find anything that went boom, or...?"

Kelly took another swig of beer. "No."

"Yet you still do it," she said, trying to suppress a laugh.

"It pays the bills."

"Look." The waitress returned with their food. "People die every day in bed, freak accidents, exercising, playing football. We're in the gaming business. The only thing we have to worry about is bad publicity."

"I think what happened to Marcy Collins is more than bad publicity."

"I didn't mean it that way." Farrell's eyes turned inward; her reply softer, respectful. "Jason Atwater is a very generous individual. He makes friends easily. Highly intelligent. Hates politics. He contributes generously to various charities both here and abroad. Although he abhors politics, he likes being seen with them. DreamQwest is his whole life."

"What about you?" said Kelly.

"I was assistant district attorney for the city of Chicago. I almost turned the DreamQwest job down."

"Why didn't you?"

"For the same reason you accepted your assignment. I was at the airport waiting to board a flight to Houston. He made me an offer."

"Atwater seems to like airports."

"He can be very convincing." Farrell took a slice of the Kielbasa. "Marcy Collins has a brother, you know. Nearly inseparable I hear."

"What happens if and when he makes an appearance?"

"By tomorrow you'll be in Washington—right?"

"That's the plan," he said, sampling the Golumpkies, washing it down with beer. "What about Ben? Where does he fit in?"

"Ben?"

"My gut tells me the relationship between him and Ben is a bit more than just employee-employer."

"Jason and Ben go back years. Ben worked with Jason's grandfather when Jason was still in college. He owns degrees in both microbiology and physics. When grandfather Atwater died, Jason was left with a rough outline of the concept behind Big Red. Ben joined him not long after that. He was the one who made it all work. Ben also developed the formula—Two Seven Five."

"Ben should know what happened. Right?"

"If he can't, no one can," she said, glancing at her watch.

"Sooner I hope," said Kelly, washing his lunch down with a swig of beer.

"I can't leave without it."

"Our competition would like nothing better than to see us fail."

Kelly remembered the supermarket tabloids a few years back floating the idea that Big Red was an alien plot to take over the world and that Dream-Qwest was a secret alien base.

"I had a V-R party one night. "It was fun. But I wouldn't recommend playing over beer."

"I wouldn't recommend doing anything over beer," she said.

"What I'm trying to say is what if Collins had a Chardonnay before getting into her Big Red?"

"If she did, it wasn't in the autopsy report."

The waitress came by to check on them. "How was lunch?"

Kelly gave her a quick smile. "Haven't tasted food this great since I was in Philly."

"Please thank Anna for us," said Farrell.

The waitress set a plate down on the table with the bill and left. Kelly reached for his wallet. Farrell grabbed the bill out of his hand.

"Compliments of DreamQwest Corporation," she said, not meaning it.

"How come your boss isn't a gamer?"

"Who told you that?"

"Jason said he never played any of his games; that he preferred living in the real world."

"God only knows what the real world is for Jason Atwater," she said. "He lives in Tower One on the fourteenth floor not mentioning the seven other floors. Twelve thousand square feet in all. It comes with a home theater, an Olympic-size pool, an atrium that looks like a tropical rain forest complete with monkeys and birds. A shooting range, and a small army of attendants. You saw Nicole. There are five just like her on the fourteenth floor."

Kelly's Ultra sounded a calvary charge. It was Billy Paul.

"You sittin' down?"

"Just had lunch."

"So did Chapman. He just ate his gun. Right there in his damn office."

Kelly's mind went south.

"Jennings called. You 're to get your ass to Washington."

"Who's Jennings?"

"Remember that stupid-looking geek in archive?"

"Fourth floor. By the cooler?"

"That one. He's your new boss."

Kelly never really knew Peter Chapman. How could he? He was nothing more than a voice over the phone with the obligatory photos of himself decorating Homeland's hallways smiling disingenuously. The final indignation was the way Chapman chose to end his tenure.

"What's wrong?" asked Farrell.

"Tell Jason to have Big Red ready when we get there. I gotta go."

The weather wasn't much different when he de-planed at Reagan. As luck would have it, a winter storm front was moving up the Atlantic seaboard. Snow was already heavy in the D.C. area as Kelly fought his way through Capitol traffic in his hybrid rental toward the Department of Homeland Security.

Not exactly a homecoming.

Kelly barely recognized the man behind the desk. Karl Jennings had put on some weight since he last remembered the geek.

Kelly and Billy Paul were preparing for transfer to a new Homeland assignment in Seattle called Product. Division. Jennings was working records at the time, cursing the powers-that-be why they hadn't recognized his potential. Except for the cleaning people, most ignored him. It was difficult to believe he was now sitting behind Chapman's over-sized desk as deputy director of homeland security. His nose had to hurt.

"Have Agent Kelly take a seat," Jennings told the security officer, as if Jennings couldn't tell him himself.

Kelly knew the type. It wasn't hard. Employees like Jennings made up the core of Washington's cadre of potential supervisory personnel who now found himself over his head as deputy director of homeland security.

Chapman's replacement apparently was too important to trust to someone with experience. Like all appointments, temporary or permanent, it wasn't based so much on proven ability but who kissed better butt.

In any case his job wasn't destined to be long-lived.

Most likely once a new president was sworn in Jennings would be replaced by someone more to the new president's liking. That went for a good quarter of Homeland's lower and middle management who'd be looking for a new job.

On the wall directly behind Jennings were the obligatory portraits of the current president and vice president of the United States, the present director, along with Peter Chapman's sullen face, apparently the powers-that-be hadn't bothered to replace with Jennings' photo until the new team in January made that decision for them. What never changed was the American flag standing immaculate on a polished brass standard along with the official Homeland seal, fixed large and ornate on the wall directly behind Jennings.

Kelly set the Big Red down on the desk. Jennings looked at him.

"What took you so long?"

"The bureau wanted it logged in at evidence custodian in Chicago," said Farris. "Agent Kelly was assigned to take the device the rest of the way to Washington."

Kelly took out a wrinkled property receipt and flattened it out on Jenning's unlittered desk. "Mission accomplished."

Agent Farris picked it up and passed it on to Jennings. "It's good."

"Why wasn't I given a heads up!" Jennings complained.

"Head's up?" said Kelly. "That's a joke—right?"

Jennings tore out a two-page report from a folder and held it up in a clenched fist. "How come everybody knows what's going on around here but me?"

"Why don't you ask 'em," said Kelly. "My job's done."

"And what *is* your job?"

"Product Division. Seattle. In case you don't know, it's part of Homeland."

Jennings put his hand on the Big Red. "This is a domestic product."

"Yes, sir."

"Product Division deals in imports."

"Correct, sir"

Jennings lifted off his chair holding between his palsied hands a bold red headline. "It's all right here in *Expose!* "

"That's a rag, sir."

"Are you aware Eleanor Chapman is accusing Homeland of covering up an illicit affair between her husband, Peter J. Chapman, and a federal prosecutor who just happened to turn up dead in Chicago?"

"What's that have to do with me, sir?"

"How does this sound? The Deputy Secretary of Homeland Security dispatches one of his most trusted agents to remove evidence from his dead girlfriend's apartment."

"Wrong. I was sent to Chicago to take possession of a device," said Kelly, glancing over at Farris. "And transport same to Chapman here in Washington."

"He's right," Farris replied. "The Bureau instructed me to log it in as an object of interest. Agent Kelly was to take it the rest of the way to Washington."

"Object of interest."

"Correct," said Farris.

"You were in her apartment," said Jennings.

"Yes. There was no evidence of foul play. The case has since been classified as a sudden death."

Jennings exhaled in frustration.

"According to what I have in front of me, your primary duty, Agent Kelly, is the inspection of imported electronic products entering the

United States that may represent a threat to national security. True?"

"That's my job description—yes."

"You also understand it is a clear violation of homeland policy to involve yourself in any investigation involving a domestic product."

"I wasn't investigating anything. I was directed by deputy director Peter J. Chapman to pick up a device in F-B-I custody and transport same to Homeland, sir."

"Anything else you wish to add?" said Jennings.

"I'm taking the Giants over Washington this Sunday."

Jennings eyes rolled back in his head. "Okay. It's out of my hands. I'm kicking this upstairs."

"This *is* upstairs."

Kelly was no lawyer. One had to be a barrister of sorts to cut through the bureaucratic language; to read between the lines of human communication the translation of which depended on what was not said. The real world was back in Seattle. Washington DC was Never-Never-Land where nothing said was what was never meant.

"When's the viewing?"

The question took Jennings by surprise. "Saturday. Ten o'clock. In Arlington." Calm was back in Jennings' voice as he reached for his mug of tepid coffee. "Closed casket from what I hear. You're on suspension until further notice."

Kelly ejected the ready round on his Sig Sauer along with the magazine and set them down on Jennings' desk.

"My badge too if you want it," he said reaching into his back pocket.

"That won't be necessary," said Jennings. "But I'll need your Ultra."

Jennings opened a drawer and took out Kelly's obsolete cell phone along with its power cord and laid them out on his desk.

"You might want to charge it."

"The rumor's true," said Kelly.

"What's that?"

"You're an asshole."

Jennings glanced over at Alec Farris. "Anything you want to add?"

"The bureau recommends Mr. Kelly keep us appraised of his whereabouts pending final determination of the case."

Kelly hated the thought of staying a whole weekend among the political elite. He also felt a lot lighter without his Sig. Washington DC wasn't exactly Chicago, but it was a close third. Like most law enforcement professionals, he had taken his weapon for granted much of the time. Like wearing aftershave. It was a life he had known close to twenty years.

The federal government, like any central authority, had a union obliged to provide a government attorney to any employee facing investigation. Kelly had the feeling he would need one. They couldn't discipline Chapman because he was dead, though Kelly doubted they would have had he lived; scandals of Chapman's nature weren't exactly rare in Washington D.C. and easily covered up. In Kelly's case, Deputy Secretary Jennings was determined to go the extra mile. Conduct unbecoming seemed like a safe bet. Nothing more than a slap on the wrist. But it was enough to threaten any future promotions. That alone would put him on a short leash.

What mattered now was the level of interest a government-supplied attorney would have in defending him should he wind up in federal court fighting not only for his job, but perhaps his freedom as well.

Win or lose, a government lawyer got paid regardless of the outcome.

His cell phone told him he had an incoming call. "Kelly!" he said, almost dropping it.

"*I must say, your phone is somewhat outdated. It took my sources a while to find you. What happened to your Ultra?*"

"I'm on suspension "

"*I somehow feel responsible for your predicament.*"

"Oh, I'm a big boy, Jason. I can take care of myself."

"*Is that so. My sources tell me you may be in need of legal representation.*"

"Part of my benefits package."

"A government attorney. Correct me if I'm wrong."

"Look. Can we discuss this some other time, Jason? I'm on my way to a viewing."

"I believe that's tomorrow. How about Ann Arbor Michigan for the moment?"

"Ann Arbor?"

"One of our corporate jets is set to leave Reagan for Kalamazoo Battle Creek International in about an hour. Ann Arbor is our corporate safehouse. Quite necessary, I'm afraid."

"Hey, look—"

"My sources tell me a federal warrant for your arrest is quite possible within the next forty-eight hours. Just show your I.D. at the corporate terminal."

It was cold and dark, close to nine o'clock, when Kelly noticed the flashing headlights behind a line of cars waiting outside arrivals in Kalamazoo, Michigan. Its distinctive front grill gave it away. It was a Mercedes Benz.

"You have to be kidding," he said in one breath.

The passenger window powered down as he walked over to meet it.

"Get in—it's freezing!" Farrell shouted.

Kelly dumped his bag in the back seat and got in.

"Moonlighting?"

"I'm your Guardian Angel," she said sarcastically "At least until tomorrow. Don't ask me why."

"You missed me. I can tell."

"If it were up to me—"

"How come I believe you?"

CHAPTER SIX

The safehouse was about an hour east of Battle Creek: a converted two-story farmhouse according to Brenda Farrell, although Kelly couldn't make out everything in the dark save for a single square of light from a first floor window. The car's headlights soon revealed a set of wooden steps leading up to a porch as Farrell pulled onto a dirt driveway with dark things jumping in and out of the headlights.

"Cats are out again," Farrell complained, slamming the car in park, beating Kelly to the high steps like some kid who scored all A's on her report card.

"Where the hell have you been, girl?" greeted an older woman.

Kelly noticed the motorized wheelchair as he stomped his shoes on the porch.

Farrell gave her a kiss. "This is Frank Kelly, Mother."

"Hello, Frank. I'm Kimberly." She looked him over, trying to read the man her daughter just brought in out of the cold. "You look tired."

"It's been a rough day," he said.

The living room resembled an antiques museum resting on a thick Persian rug with two overly plush couches and a recliner facing the warmth of a stone fireplace, a rustic clock keeping time on a shelf above the warmth of glowing embers.

The recliner looked comfortable enough to sleep on.

"House is much too big for this old dame," said Kimberly.

She was an older version of her daughter. Except for the grey hair, the difference wasn't really all that much. The resemblance between them was close enough to pass for sisters. More often than not daughters looked like their fathers, and sons their mothers—at least it seemed that way according to the Farmer's Almanac.

"Be careful," said Farrell. "Mom's a psychiatrist."

Kelly noticed the framed degrees on the wall above the stone fireplace along with a huge University of Michigan faculty award certificate.

"You're going to scare the pants off this handsome young man," said Kimberly. "And I barely know him," tossing a small log onto the glowing embers. "Whiskey, beer, or wine?"

"Uh, I'll have a beer," said Kelly, more tired than thirsty.

"For a brief moment I thought you came to tell me you finally found the right man," Kimberly half whispered on her way to the kitchen.

"Seriously, Mother! Frank has some legal problems. Jason thought it best we keep him out of sight."

"What did he do?" said Kimberly, taking a long neck bottle of beer out of the fridge, handing it to her daughter.

"Politics, Mother."

Kimberly shook her head. "They ought to clean that whole place up," she said, speeding off to the other side of the living room to a liquor cabinet.

"Still drinking Vodka Martinis, daughter?"

Brenda handed Kelly his beer. "Go easy on the vodka, Mother— and don't forget the olives."

"We're out of olives, dear."

"Why didn't you call me!"

"So, dear. What happened? I thought we were going to spend the week end together?" Kimberly handed Brenda her drink and wheeled around in front of the fireplace warming a small glass of Brandy.

"It's complicated, Mother."

"When you make the kind of money Jason Atwater makes someone's going to want a slice of that pie. It's human nature."

"It's not like that at all, Mother."

"Could have fooled me. Doing business today is like navigating a minefield on a pogo stick." Kimberly turned and faced Kelly. "You hungry, Frank?"

"Tired more than anything, Kimberly."

"Well, let me know when you've had enough. Daughter here will take you to bed."

"Mother!"

A black cat ran out of the kitchen and jumped up onto Kimberly's lap.

"This little girl's name is Hazel."

Brenda arched her eyebrows. "Appropriately named. Mother has a dozen cats. Hazel is her favorite."

"Don't lie to the man, dear. I have three, and they're all beautiful little darlings. The rest are feral. But I love them all."

"So, you once taught," said Kelly looking up again at the certificates on the wall above the fireplace.

"Evolutionary psychology—still do, Frank."

It was the way she said it. Kelly wrongly assumed Kimberly was retired. Wheelchair and all. He felt like an ass. Words were like bullets—can't get them back once out of the barrel.

"Sounds like a pretty heavy subject," said Kelly.

"It's not as impenetrable as it sounds, young man. Human psychological traits relating to language, memory, and perception." One look at Kelly and she knew she had already lost him. "Have you ever had a hunch about something, Frank?"

"You mean a gut feeling."

"Humans acquired certain survival traits based on accumulative experiences in the remote past—though not to be confused with instinct."

"I thought they were one and the same."

"The kind I'm talking about is acquired."

"I took a few psychology classes. U-C-L-A Berkeley."

"Did you. My classes are mostly for graduate students in pursuit of doctorates. Evolutionary psychology is a very interesting subject once you understand the basics."

"Mine was job related."

"Which is?"

"Law enforcement."

Kimberly Farrell looked deeply about what she wanted to say next.

"I once testified in court for the city of Detroit in a wrongful death suit involving one of their police officers. The officer was cleared of criminal charges, but that didn't stop the family from suing him civilly. The officer's original testimony cited probable cause when he approached a possible suspect he recognized from a previous arrest.

"Basically, the officer relied on his experience based on the fact the suspect had an extensive criminal history. At point of contact, the suspect was wearing a full-length trench coat with an object visibly protruding from his coat despite the fact it was summer. The officer, believing it may be a weapon ordered him to the ground. The man did not comply. The officer shot the man multiple times as he reached under his coat."

"A shotgun?"

"Well—no," said Kimberly. "It was a piece of pipe."

"Most bank tellers wouldn't argue with that," said Kelly.

"Would you have shot him?" she asked.

"Considering he had a criminal history my survival instincts would've taken over. It's a possibility."

"A fifty-fifty proposition. You only need to be wrong once." She took a quick sip of brandy and continued. "Humans are at the bottom of the list when it comes to instinct," she said stroking Hazel's rich, black fur. "We humans are not good at it. Instinct doesn't come naturally to us. We aren't as developed as the rest of the animal kingdom. It's a lot more subtle. We need a lot more information. By then it's usually too late."

"Contrary to popular myth," said Kelly. "Not all police officers have good instincts."

Kimberly hugged her brandy. "I agree. Then there's perception."

"Perception?"

"You're sitting at your computer revising a paper you wrote a week ago," she began, noticing Brenda's eyes arch sharply upward. "You've written six pages and you look up at the clock and find two hours have passed."

Kelly trumped her. "What if you stared at that same clock for a few minutes without blinking? You would think an hour had passed—yeah, I get that."

"Both are perceptions. It's how we perceive reality."

"You lost me."

Farrell looked down into her Martini. "You should have told me you needed olives, Mother."

"In the thirteenth century," Kimberly went on to explain, "people didn't have watches, clocks, or computers. They had sundials, hourglasses, and water clocks. The clock, invented in the early fourteenth century mainly served merchants and tradesmen to keep track of shipment schedules to determine profits and losses."

"Get to the point, Mother."

"Sundials were useless on cloudy days. People had to look up and guess where the Sun was, whether it was *before* noon, or *after* noon—noon meaning the center of the sky if you look straight up— according to the sun's approximate position in the sky. For ordinary people it didn't really matter. Things changed when the clock was invented."

A curious thought struck Kelly. "Would this same theory apply if I were playing Garden of Eden?"

"What on earth are you talking about?" said Kimberly.

"It's a DreamQwest game, Mother," Brenda moaned. "He has a fixation about sex."

"Oh, that's right," said Kimberly in curious afterthought. "I don't believe I ever played that one. But I can see your point. One's perception of time is indeed different during game play."

"When I'm playing Pro Golf 2016," said Brenda. "All concept of time disappears."

"And your golf game?" said Kelly.

"I'm not saying DreamQwest will make you a better golfer. The most common complaint from our customers is that they think they automatically become experts at whatever game they play. It doesn't work that way."

"Do tell us, daughter."

"Played African Safari once—never since," Brenda confessed. "I selected a twenty-two rifle from a pre-game list of guns. Had a great hunting guide, too."

"A pop gun," Kelly smirked.

"Anyway, this Rhino sees me and charges. He was so close I could feel his breath...."

"Oh, my. What happened?" Kimberly gasped.

"I closed my eyes for fifteen seconds and got the hell out of the game."

"Coward."

"What if he'd caught up to you?" Kelly teased.

Brenda took a sip of her Vodka Martini and shrugged. "Game over—I guess."

"Just curious."

Kimberly looked over at Kelly with amused suspicion. "What are you getting at, young man?"

"Well, if Big Red games are as real as people think they are—"

"I know where you're going with this," said Brenda. "But you've never played. You have to play to know what you're talking about."

"My favorite is Travel World," said Kimberly. "It's fantastic. It lets me travel anywhere in the world from the comfort of my wheelchair." She looked over at Kelly. "We all need a break from reality once in a while."

"I prefer the here and now."

"Mr. Kelly's into toys, Mother."

"Oh, heavens. Well, let me tell you. Big Red is as real as you and I sitting here right now young man. I remember my entire trip to Europe. It was a gorgeous day in France. I found this beautiful outdoor café in Paris. I remember ordering a huge glass of Chardonnay with a distinguished looking gentleman giving me the eye from a far table."

"Sights. Sounds?"

"Perfectly real. The scenario is still fresh in my mind."

"The wine? Could you taste it?" he asked.

Kimberly had to think about that one. "I don't want to say I could. Would anyone remember the taste of anything from the day before?"

"So you can't," said Kelly.

"For want of a better description, it was more like a vivid dream," she replied. "They're quite real, you know."

"The only thing that stands out in my dreams are the commercials," Kelly confessed.

Kimberly wheeled closer to him. "Commercials?"

"I always get these stupid commercial breaks—toothpaste, I think."

Only the spit and crackle of the fireplace could be heard above the profound silence that followed as mother and daughter exchanged glances.

"I believe the poor boy's tired," said Kimberly, looking foolish for almost believing him as Brenda laughed quietly to herself.

"You're right," Kelly confessed. "I'm tired."

Kimberly wheeled over and eased the beer out of his hand. "Brenda will show you to your room sweetheart."

"This way, Frank," said Brenda, grabbing his backpack. Kelly followed her to the staircase leading up to the second floor. She stopped when they got near the top. The hallway was long, narrow, and barely lit. "Your room's second door on the right."

"You coming to tuck me in?" he said, passing her by one step.

"It's getting late, daughter!" Kimberly's voice cried out from below.

"Coming, Mother." Brenda looked up at Kelly before heading down. "I warn you—we're early birds."

*   *   *

She wasn't kidding.

"Frank—wake up!"

Kelly glanced at his watch from a bed two sizes too small in a room made for a ten-year-old. He fell asleep only because he was too tired not to. Brenda poked him again.

"It's four-thirty," he complained, rubbing his face. "You guys get up this early every Sunday?"

"Keep your voice down!" she snapped as she would a two-year-old.

"Mom's sleeping! Get dressed! Jason called. We have to go."

"I have to shower—"

"We don't have time. Put some clothes on."

"I don't have to," he said, throwing off the covers "I never took 'em off."

CHAPTER SEVEN

Jason was behind his desk when Farrell and Kelly joined the meeting-in-progress; only no one was talking. The atmosphere in the office was palpably subdued. Something wasn't right.

"Sorry," said Farrell, "Roads were really bad."

Atwater nodded compliantly, the usual glass of milk and a tray of chocolate donut holes in front of him untouched, wearing only a sweatshirt and blue jeans. Totally out of character. Then again, Kelly didn't know all the sides of Jason Atwater.

"Coffee?" Atwater offered with the wave of a hand, indicating a small table set with a carafe of coffee, some cups, and a warm basket of cheese croissants. Kelly grabbed a coffee and seated himself next to Farrell.

Ben Nettlebaum was there as well, sitting almost unnoticed to the left of Atwater, adjusting his Ben Franklins.

The absence of classical music added to the overall despondency in the room.

"Ben has come to some conclusions regarding the Big Red," said Atwater. "You may proceed with your report, Ben."

Nettlebaum adjusted his glasses, resting them on the bridge of his nose.

"The data disc from Marcy Collins Big Red was analyzed," he began slowly, unsure of what he wanted to say. "It was empty of all content."

"Wait a minute," said Farrell. "All forty hours?"

"Nothing. Had Ms. Collins been sharing her scenarios, there would have been some preparation by Ms. Collins on her data disc. There was nothing. It appears the disk was deleted."

Kelly looked over at Atwater. "What's sharing?"

"It is a term our customers use when one participant willingly allows another player to participate in a scenario. In this case there was nothing."

"Who else had access to Collins' Big Red?" said Farrell.

"Originally I was to take possession from F-B-I Agent Alec Farris at the crime scene in Collins' condo and deliver it personally to Peter Chapman at Homeland Security."

"Did you?" said Farrell

"No. According to Agent Farris he was instructed by his superiors to turn the device over to the Chicago police department evidence custodian."

Farrell laughed in frustration. "So much for chain of evidence."

"I agree," said Kelly. "Pretty sloppy police work."

"So, anyone could have altered it," Atwater concluded. "The device we had in our possession may not be Collins' Big Red."

"A distinct possibility," replied Nettlebaum. "Which means the device's data disk I copied from the one Mr. Kelly brought us was useless."

Jason Atwater wrung his hands in disgust. "So we have nothing."

"If we could obtain Peter Chapman's device," said Farrell. "At least we would know there was a relationship going on between Chapman and Collins."

Kelly got up and poured himself another coffee. "What if she hands it over to the F-B-I?"

"Even if Quantico agreed," said Ben Nettlebaum, "they wouldn't have the proper equipment or technology to evaluate the evidence."

Kelly's cell phone warbled a pathetic bleat. It was Billy Paul.

"Yeah, B-P. What's up?"

"I checked that item you asked me about. What Jason Atwater said is true. They make everything at DreamQwest, including the neo-lithiums. No subsidiaries. No foreign interests. Everything is made right here in the good-old U-S-A."

"Thanks, B-P."

"Look. Sorry to hear about your suspension…"

"Crap rolls down hill, Billy. I just happened to be at the bottom."

"So. You had me investigated," said Atwater, a sardonic smile creasing his young face.

"Had to do it, Jason. He was just a little late getting back to me."

"Had I been in your position I probably would have done the same."

Kelly admired the young man; though at first meeting he was somewhat skeptical; nothing more than a rich kid with a name and a few billion dollars. That he had taken a theory, an idea, and created one of the most successful gaming products since Windows was an astonishing accomplishment for anyone at any age.

Atwater got up slowly. "I thank you for the presentation, Ben."

"If I may add, sir," said Ben, putting his glasses back on. "I agree it would be most helpful if we had Mr. Chapman's Big Red."

"Look. If you'll excuse me, I have a funeral to go to," said Kelly.

"Of course, Frank. Ms. Farrell here will take you to the airport."

For a brief moment Kelly had the impression Atwater had something else he wanted to say.

"Ready?" said Farrell, dangling a set of car keys in front of him.

*   *   *

Three and a half hours later Kelly was in Washington on his way to Arlington, Virginia. He had caught the tail end of a news report on his rental's dashboard TV. Most of the noise was nothing more than political posturing of which Washington was famous. But what he did learn was that DreamQwest was being urged to testify before Congress. The pressure was on. DreamQwest, they predicted, could face sanctions, or even prosecution; most owing their allegiance to companies most affected by DreamQwest. No one, however, especially Congress, wanted to kill off a 350 billion dollar corporation and risk the ire of devout followers both here and abroad. Such a move would be politically painful.

Kelly had done some research on his own.

It turned out seventy-four percent of Big Red users would remain staunchly loyal to the company, as opposed to 15% that would take a wait-and-see approach with 10% demanding a full refund if Big Red, and by extension DreamQwest, was found to be negligent.

Negative publicity was never a good thing especially a business as popular as DreamQwest. Like any organization, it survived on its reputation, living day to day in the public trust.

The publicity surrounding Marcy Collins' death was predictable, if unwanted.

The Arlington neighborhood was typically middle class—not that it mattered to Kelly. He also knew Peter Chapman long enough to know middle class was not his venue.

The funeral parlor was small and quaint. Low key seemed to be the priority. Small wood frame with a folksy white porch front facade, the proper wreaths displayed on its double doors. Parking, it seemed, was limited to maybe twenty cars.

Kelly counted eleven. Not a good sign. Two of them S-U-V Suburbans, all sleek and black. Secret Service?

In any case it was obvious the Chapman family had opted for a low-key affair. The less attention the better.

Kelly parked his rental and walked quickly toward the funeral parlor's main entrance.

"Agent Kelly—or is it Mister now?"

Kelly turned to meet the voice.

An elderly gentleman dressed in a long black coat with a tuff of silver hair so thick it made his head seem larger than it was, both hands buried deep in the pockets of an expensive full-length fleece-lined wool coat.

"Senator Arthur Bell of Oklahoma," the man boasted. "As if that matters."

"Well, I'll be damned." said Kelly. "It's been a while, Senator."

Kelly once had been assigned to the senator's protection detail in Tulsa, Oklahoma during the latter's campaign tour when Kelly worked Secret Service. It involved a nut case with a knife. Kelly had used the necessary force, and then some, to subdue the individual and bring the situation under control. The Press, of course, excoriated Kelly for using excessive force but since squashed by the senator. In fact Bell invited him to a barbecue at his home on the outskirts of Oklahoma City as compensation for saving his life.

"I never forget a face, Agent Kiley."

"*Kelly*, sir. Two 'L's'."

Senator Bell accompanied Kelly the rest of the way to the parlor's doors.

"I didn't know you knew Pete Chapman," said Bell.

"I didn't—at least not personally. I was transferred to Product Division back in twenty-six."

"Neither did I. At least not well enough to brag about it. Those who did know him didn't want the negative publicity of being seen with him. I'm retiring in any case. I'm presently expendable."

A pair of young news people spilled from the funeral home and headed their way. One of them pushed a microphone up into Bell's face while his partner recorded the event.

"At least vultures wait a bit before gorging on a carcass," Bell declared.

"Senator. Local News Four. I'd like your comment on—"

"Be delighted, my boy," said Bell.

"I understand the commerce committee will be holding hearings on the DreamQwest question."

"Mere rumors, my boy. Congress has yet to reach a consensus on the issue."

"Is that because you have a vested interest in DreamQwest, Senator?"

Bell smiled for the camera. "I am here to pay my respects to the Chapman family," he said pushing the reporter aside. "Have a nice day."

Kelly shut off his cell phone the moment he entered the parlor, surrendering his black leather jacket to a young lady with a soft Virginia smile. He felt out of place. Mostly family and friends. All he wanted was to pay his respects and leave.

The widow, dressed in traditional black, stood flanked by two grown sons and a little girl holding fake flowers in her tiny white-gloved hands, her eyes moist and red from crying. To their right was a large photo of Peter J Chapman on display to one side of the closed bronze casket. A wall of flowers filled the space behind it. As expected, the talk was polite.

Then there was the man kneeling at the foot of the casket, rising slowly, turning to face the family, and Senator Bell, armed with a forty-five pistol.

"Gun!" Kelly yelled, instinctively reaching for his own no longer there, stepping in front of the senator as two shots rang out, followed by four more piercing the air.

The next thing Kelly saw was a man lying face down on the tile floor drowning in his own blood. It was immediately followed by the shrieks and screams of everyone in attendance.

"You okay, Senator?" said Kelly, grabbing hold of the senator's arm. He suddenly felt out of breath.

The senator caught him as he leaned forward. "You just stay down, my boy. Help's on its way."

For a brief moment Kelly had no idea what Bell was saying until he lost consciousness. By then it didn't matter.

*   *   *

Kelly had seen his share of hospitals to recognize the beeping sound: It was the electronic equivalent of a human heartbeat as performed by a monitor. He assumed it was his own since he was the only one in the curtained cubicle. It took a few labored breaths to convince himself he was alive. A bit nauseated maybe, but not dead. A nurse leaned over him like some biologist examining a bug in a jar. A second figure joined her, a face mask hanging from a male neck peering down at him with the same face-stretching curiosity as the nurse.

"How are we feeling, Mr. Kelly?"

"Like I been playing football without shoulder pads," complained Kelly

"My name is Dr. George Friedman. I am your surgeon."

Doctors always liked saying "we" as if they were somehow attached to the patient.

"I feel like puking," said Kelly.

Both surgeon and nurse took a step back.

"The effects of the anesthesia," the surgeon said, quickly placing a bedpan under his chin as the nurse injected something into one of two bags suspended on a poll above him.

He wasn't lying.

"What happened?" said Kelly.

"You were admitted to George Washington University Hospital," the surgeon explained, "gunshot wounds to the upper chest and shoulder. You lost a fair amount of blood. You are in recovery. Do you understand what I am saying?"

"What time is it?"

"It's just after six in the evening, Mr. Kelly."

Kelly's neck hurt when he tried lifting his head; a pain that went from his left shoulder to his upper chest heavily packed in bandages. His left arm had been immobilized in a hard sling with an I-V stuck in his right arm.

"My left ear hurts," he said, wanting to cough. The queasiness in his stomach were not hunger pangs.

"Bone fragments from your left collar bone, Mr. Kelly," the surgeon said. "It took off part of your ear lobe."

"Try not moving so much," the nurse cautioned.

"What about the breathing part?"

The doctor checked the tubing going into his arm. "Bruising. You are one lucky man, Mr. Kelly. The bullets didn't hit anything vital. One of them partially shattered your left collar bone on impact. Bone splinters are like shrapnel. We were worried about your carotid. We put everything back together for you. There is some tissue damage affecting the pectoral muscles in your chest. You should be on your feet fairly quickly."

Strange what little he remembered. It angered him that he could have died without ever knowing he was dead. In all his years as a police officer, including the years spent in Treasury, he'd never taken a bullet. He thought of Senator Bell,

"Was anyone else—?"

"I cannot answer that. You were the only one admitted to this hospital, Mr. Kelly."

"How soon can I leave?"

"A week perhaps. We don't keep patients any longer than we have to."

That's what they always said. The doctor disappeared in the folds of the curtain. The nurse stayed long enough to whisper a message in his ear.

"There's a Senator Bell outside. He insists on seeing you."

Arthur Bell's deep loud voice filled the cubicle. "I hear you're going to live."

"That was part of the plan when I woke up this morning, Senator."

Bell pulled up a chair. "I won't keep you, son."

"I thought for sure you were the target."

"The shooter turned out to be someone's brother. I believe Eleanor Chapman was his target, maybe the whole family."

"Eye-for-an-eye."

"I was standing in front of her when you alerted us. Secret Service took care of the rest."

The image of a black SUV rolled across his brain. The one following his cab in Chicago. The one he noticed out in the parking lot before...

"The F-B-I's reopening the investigation," Bell added. "Eleanor Chapman has already hired an arsenal of lawyers."

"Chapman's wife? What for?"

"The government." The senator unbuttoned his heavy coat. It still had blood on it—-Kelly's blood. "I heard about your suspension. Jennings, as you already know, is an asshole of the first order."

"So, what's next?"

"You will be in need of an attorney, son," said Bell. "The reason I came by was to thank you. Scandals are for tabloids, my boy. Your boss made the mistake of mixing sex and politics."

Kelly's stitches were starting to itch. Nothing worse than an itch you can't scratch.

"The question I have is why you were there at all?" said Bell.

"A personal decision," said Kelly. "I had some questions of my own."

"You don't seem to understand, my boy. You're last man standing. There's a media circus heading your way. The other thing I need tell you is DreamQwest ain't too big to fail like some people think."

"What are you telling me?"

The senator pumped himself up pompously. "The only true loser in this whole mess is you. Jason is that new breed of wealthy entrepreneurs who don't believe in politics. Or money. Genius for its own sake is a waste of time."

Kelly didn't need a Core lesson in math to figure out where Arthur Bell was coming from.

"The Commerce Committee is scheduled to meet on DreamQwest fairly soon," the senator continued. "Jason Atwater might want to take it seriously."

A muted buzzing sound announced itself between Kelly's legs. The senator removed the offending cell phone from a plastic bag of personal effects and handed it to him. "I didn't know they made cell phones anymore."

Kelly recognized the voice.

Senator Bell got up slowly. "I'll be going now," he said quietly. "Let me know if there's anything I can do."

"For someone trying to keep a low profile you're doing a shitty job."
It was Brenda Farrell
"I had to pay my respects."
"Suspended treasury agent involved in shooting at Arlington funeral home. It's all over the news. You could have been killed!"
A phlebotomist sauntered into the room carrying a tray.
"Listen, one of Dracula's kids just came in to take my blood."
"Has anyone interviewed you yet?"
"They just wheeled me out of surgery. I don't even know who shot me."
"It was Collins' brother! It's on all the networks. Listen. Let me talk to Jason. Don't do anything stupid!"
"I already did."
An hour later they wheeled him out of post-op into a private room.
Three suits were waiting for him. One was his government appointed attorney. The other two were federal agents. Neither was glad to see him.

CHAPTER EIGHT

"Sarge—take a look at this." a Denver police department detective said leaning over a report on his desk. His sergeant was bald and smelled of onions. He snatched the report out of the detective's hand.

"Whataya got?"

"Uniform got a call at eight-oh-five this morning. Patricia Delaney age twenty-four said she was raped. I have her affidavit right here."

"The Perp?" The sergeant looked up at the clock above the coffee table thinking about he was going to have for lunch.

"No perp, Sarge. It was someone she met online. They were playing Survival. She was allegedly raped during game play."

"During game play."

"What do we do with it, Sarge?"

"Big Red's a lot like Vegas. What happens in Vegas stays in Vegas.

"Yeah, I know, but—"

"The judge will throw it out."

Survival, and the dozen or so other DreamQwest games on the market, were nothing more than entertainment after all. Players create their own cast of characters and scenarios. Oddly enough, sex crimes had dropped by fifty percent, all due to Big Red.

"I like Dinosaur Hunt myself," said the detective. "Family loves it."

"Ever get eaten?" said the sergeant, grabbing a menu from a top drawer.

"If I don't like what's going down all I gotta do is close my eyes for a few seconds—poof. It's back to reality. She could have done the same. File it."

*   *   *

Billy Paul wanted to enjoy a nice hot shower and a change of clothes; not that it made a difference since the scenario called for a tuxedo. He could be naked for all that it mattered.

Game four was tonight. His Swedish soccer team was leading 2-1 in the championship series, and he wanted to be in feel-good shape. The Mavericks, the opposing team in the playoffs, despite having lost the first two games, were still dangerous. The last thing he wanted was to let himself and the girls get overconfident. He also created his scenario to be more competitive using random mode. More fun. More natural.

He noticed the porch timer lights were out again on his quaint two-story porch front home of Greenwood in Seattle's old town, checking the mailbox on his way up the narrow concrete walkway to the porch. The last time he got home this late the neighborhood kids slipped a plastic spider in his mailbox. Finding no surprises this time, he fished out the usual assortment of bills and junk mail, slowly climbing the steps, stumbling over a package on his way in.

Ripping open the outer packaging, he found it was the book he ordered two weeks ago: Decoding the Infinite by Nigel Atwater. He had the entire collection now.

Holographic Reality had been Nigel Atwater's first book. A largely obscure book and hard to find. Mostly about what holography was about than anything else. And how it could be applied. Billy Paul thought it more a master plan, a manifesto more than a scientific treatise on the future of holographic reality; a master plan for the reconditioning of the human psyche.

Billy Paul cursed himself as he set the book down on a small antique table next to a vase with no flowers. Terry, his deceased wife of fifty-two years had always kept flowers in that particular vase with its rose clusters and antique designs. But creep into his mind it did. Life had never been the same without her.

Billy Paul walked into the kitchen and opened the fridge pulling out a long bottle by its neck. He had to clear his mind.

Tonight would decide the playoffs. It was the biggest game of his make-believe life. He set the beer down on the coffee table next to a recliner and sat down thinking about his girls.

*   *   *

A nurse came by Kelly's room the next morning to tell him he had another visitor.

"It's a Mrs. Chapman."

Kelly raised his head slightly and felt the stabbing pain in his shoulder. He didn't like pain pills. He had seen too many junkies in his life to start popping for every itch and throb. Besides, pain killers made him constipated.

Had the rounds impacted a few inches slightly south of his right nipple he'd be wearing a toe tag. At least the pain told him he was alive. He pushed his bowl of cereal aside. His stomach wasn't in the mood for goat food.

Kelly wasn't in the mood for visitors either.

The woman was on the beefy side, but otherwise quite attractive. She approached slowly, tentatively, sizing him up with every advancing footstep still dressed in black, the black vail covering her face failing to hide a different kind of hurt.

"I am Eleanor Chapman."

The question Kelly had was why Chapman's wife would even bother after everything she'd been through. Kinda creepy. Pete Chapman had never once mentioned her in conversation. Kelly searched for the right words. He was never much good at condolences, especially the wife of a dead boss he thought he knew but didn't.

"The shooter is dead," she said, smiling, moving closer. "Was it you who killed him?"

Who was keeping score?

*   *   *

In retrospect, Kelly never knew or met the man and couldn't pick him out of a lineup if his life depended on it. Even now his memory of yesterday's event was a blur of bodies seeking cover and the smell of cologne on Senator Bell's coat.

Anyway, he didn't need any more memories.

Kelly had his own problems. Mostly assurances from his government- -appointed attorney that the situation was well in hand. What he wanted to know was for which side? Hell, the attorney couldn't even tell him what the pending charges were but hinted they could be obstruction of justice, and tampering with evidence? The fact the federal bureau had dropped its investigation into Marcy Collins death as nothing more than natural. The coroner's office for the state of Illinois cleared everyone, directly or indirectly, with her death, at least for the moment.

The charges against Kelly was a different matter. The fact he was in possession of possible evidence when Peter Chapman ended his life had raised some red flags. Jennings, his incompetent replacement, wanted everyone in Washington to know he was a player.

"I'm sorry for your loss," he said. "It must be—"

"Oh, spare me the grief." Eleanor Chapman replied. "Peter wasn't much of a man even when the sonofabitch was alive."

So much for the sympathy card.

"Peter liked you," she continued. "He was quite jealous of you in fact— afraid you'd take his job."

That Chapman had confessed any such feelings to his wife was doubtful. Kelly remembered mostly the expletives.

Kelly was starting to suspect there was more to Peter Chapman than just a voice at the other end of a phone. In any case, Kelly had no idea what Chapman really thought about him, or did he care. The last time he talked with him he was being less than truthful about the assignment he'd given him. But he never wished the man dead.

As for his widow, Eleanor Chapman was typical of a Washington veteran. Kelly had seen far too many eyes during his career not to be able to read hers. In law enforcement, everything was in the eyes and hands. So far, she held nothing in her hand that suggested trouble, even though the dark hurt on Eleanor Chapman's face started to make him nervous.

"That's why he sent you to Seattle," she said, her voice rising in tone. "I wish he had spent more time with his family and not with that whore—"

"You knew—for sure?"

"Peter was on his Big Red every night! Playing that so-called game. Word gets around in this town, like who's doing who. They need to take that thing off the market!" Her hands tightened into fists. "I mean that's what that thing does."

"I don't know. I'm not a player."

"That stupid machine ruined my life and killed my husband," she said, anger rising in her voice as she stepped closer. "I need closure, Mr. Kelly."

A nurse entered the room with a cluster of red roses and placed them in a vase on a small table by the window. Kelly was glad to see her. The nurse plucked a business card from the flowers and handed it to him. It was from Brenda Farrell.

"I think I know someone who might."

*   *   *

The soccer match between the Wichita Mavericks and the Washington Big Foot went well. Although they were leading by a goal at the half, he could taste victory, sitting proudly on the bench with his girls, a Cheshire grin spreading wide on his round, cherubic face soaking up the cheers in the packed stadium.

"You realize the Mavericks are supposed to be the best soccer team in town," said the owner Eddie Paulson, a big fellow with a voice to match. "That was one hell of a first half, B-P."

"Them's my girls, Mr. Paulson!" The bench hooted back at him. "All right now!" he cackled. "The second half starts in five minutes. Let's get out there and wrap this up!"

Of course, he had loaded his team with the best players he could find in sports magazines and on-line. The rest was up to him. That's what 'random' was all about. Random was so much better than the usual easy, hard, and expert. Billy Paul thought random was more natural.

"I'm throwin' a party," said Paulson, over the shouts of his girls as they ran back onto the field. "Everyone's invited!"

Billy Paul feigned surprise. "That's mighty generous, Mr. Paulson."

"Tomorrow evening at nine. The Kingston Inn. My man will pick you up at eight."

But of course. Billy Paul wrote the script. The Kingston Inn was nothing more than a figment writ large. It didn't exist. What it came down to was a bunch of zeroes and ones. Of course, Big Red did all the math. He was merely its enabler.

Billy Paul had long ago outgrown most versions of the game. If you played long enough winning was easy even at the hardest level. What was missing was randomness.

DreamQwest's latest version hit the gaming world with an improved random factor in 2026. Like life itself, it allowed a player to design his own scenarios in the most exacting detail including personalities capable of spontaneous thought. Big Red's Quantum Engine made it all possible.

"I'll be there, Mr. Paulson. You can bet on it."

Billy Paul joined the owner at the chalk line to watch the start of the second half and, hopefully, a win.

CHAPTER NINE

"F-B-I's on their way," Farrell nervously informed him on the phone. *A warrant was issued for your arrest. The F-B-I should be there in a couple hours."*

Warrant or no warrant, he wasn't going anywhere. He knew the procedure. They would advise him of his rights, then assign an agent to his room until he was in good enough shape to transfer.

"You're going to be discharged against medical advice," Farrell explained.

Kelly wanted to laugh, but the stitches wouldn't let him.

"Tell Jason—-."

"Shut up and listen! A nurse will be up to your room shortly with some papers for you to sign."

"You realize that'll make me a fugitive."

"There'll be an ambulance waiting out front to take you to Reagan. They're going to wheel you down along with your medical records and medications. One of our corporate jets is on standby."

"The F-B-I's probably monitoring our conversation right now."

"Jason put your cell on his Ultra system. Right now you have to get ready to move."

His nurse hurried into the room a few minutes later.

"You're to take one every two hours," she said, slapping a vial of antibiotics in Kelly's palm. "No bathing or showers for at least a week. Sponge bath's okay. You'll need to have your dressing changed twice a day."

"What about beer?"

The nurse gave him a look. "Definitely not. Alcohol is a blood thinner." She nervously handed him a clipboard. "You need to sign these."

Who said money didn't talk?

Kelly scratched his signature on each of the six pages.

"Good luck to you, Mr. Kelly."

The small twin engine transport was a rear-loader and the two on-board EMS crew had little trouble wheeling him up into the belly of the plane. There were few seats. Enough for the two EMS on board and a physician dressed in a tuxedo.

"Good afternoon, Mr. Kelly. I will be your doctor on this flight."

"You're not dressed like one."

"My daughter got married today."

"I'd hate to see the bill."

"You won't. Jason Atwater will—-a big one."

Billy Paul called as the doctor took a seat next to one of the EMS.

"My fantasy team won the championship. Three to Two!"

"That's terrific," said Kelly, faking interest. His upper arm was starting to throb. "Look, I gotta go—"

"Yeah. Me too. Gotta get ready."

"Look, pal. I'll be coming out your way in a couple days."

"Everything okay?" You sound different."

"Tired."

"I'll let you know how it went," said Billy Paul.

A little over two hours later Kelly was in Ann Arbor.

*   *   *

"Daughter! I need you!" Kimberly shouted as she opened the door for the EMS, wheeling around to give them room.

"Where do you want him, Miss?" asked one of the EMS.

"There's a room under the stairway. Be careful, it has a small doorway."

"I need a beer," Kelly complained.

"You're burning up," said Kimberly, touching his forehead. "The last thing you need is beer."

Brenda Farrell was already in the room, serving once as a library, and came with a small cot her mother used from time to time to rest and read books.

"It's ready," said Farrell, guiding EMS through the doorway. A pair of pajamas waited for Kelly on a stack of books. She removed his hospital slippers as they transferred him to the cot.

"His personal affects?"

EMS handed Farrell a plastic bag. "Sign here please,"

Kimberly peeled off his hospital socks and covered him with a sheet.

"It's warm in here," said Kelly, wetting his cracked lips with his tongue.

"Mother!" she yelled. "He's seeping!"

"Feels like I just ran the mile," complained Kelly, trying to catch his breath.

"Lie down! Stop fighting me!"

"You will do as you are told young man!" boomed a deep menacing voice now taking physical form, standing a full six-foot-six inches with arms that would shame a wrestler.

"I got this," she said, setting down a black leather bag.

"Who the hell are you?" said Kelly, staring up at the huge figure looming over his bed.

"I'm Molly!"

*   *   *

It had taken Billy Paul most of the night developing the scenario for his World Cup celebration party. The team's owner, his assistants, and of course, his Swedish soccer team, were already programmed into the scenario.

Several hundred make-believe guests, including a full string orchestra along with food and beverage courts had to be created from scratch and up-loaded.

The venue itself had been an architectural nightmare: a towering twenty-eight story monstrosity of chrome steel and glass superimposed in the middle of downtown Seattle. Big Red's Quantum Assembly with its zero's and one's had done the rest.

The party began with his arrival by limo at 9:45 in the evening; although time didn't really matter. The elevator then ascended up to the ballroom enclosed in ceiling-to-floor cathedral windows overlooking the panoramic lights of Seattle twenty-eight stories above the early evening haze.

A full string orchestra playing Mozart greeted him as he stepped off onto a shallow rotating stage set with tables adorned with the finest cuisine and fountains of the best liquors populated with believable guests he had spent most of the night creating.

The believable people consisted of three tiers:

Tier One's were those designed to interact with him randomly: random-ness was so much more realistic. Tier One's were the closest to authentic people capable of open and free discussion—to a point.

Tier Two people reacted only in action and conversation with no input of their own, like those in the orchestra, and the couples now swirling about on the dance floor mimicking some giant music box.

Tier Three people were the waiters and greeters with no special ability other than to serve and greet and say nice things even when provoked.

Billy Paul realized the moment he stepped out onto the ballroom floor that he had slightly overdone it. The scene reminded out of an early twentieth century musical.

Definitely overstated.

"Good evening, Coach Stevens," cooed an attractive young woman wearing red flowers dressed in a bright yellow evening gown held up with spaghetti straps. "You look so wonderful tonight."

Tier Three. Official greeter.

Billy Paul had cut her out of a science fiction fantasy magazine and scanned her into his scenario. Tier Threes were the most numerous and less time consuming to create. Those now populating the ballroom floor added to the overall illusion and nothing more. Some were duplicates. Laziness on his part. He had already spotted a few look-a-likes as he made his way through the crowded ballroom. By this time tomorrow all would be archived. Maybe a world tour with his soccer team would be next on his agenda.

"Well, if it isn't coach of the year Billy Paul Stevens!" greeted George, one of his in-game assistant coaches. A Tier Two. George was a quiet man normally somewhere in the background during games mostly because he was irrelevant, now standing stark naked with a drink in one hand and the other around a girl with no hair.

"Oops—looks like I forgot something, George," he laughed. "My mistake. Have fun."

George raised his drink in a high salute and smiled, then mixed with the other Tier Twos.

"Have fun!"

Of course, all were mere figments of his scenario brought to life by the miracle of Big Red.

Billy spotted his Tier One Swedish World Cup team over by the food court posing in full uniform to an audience of eager Tier Three photographers.

"Over here, boys!" exclaimed Eddie Paulson, the team owner, decked out in purple leotards, golf shoes with long red hair down to his elbows wearing a Che Guevara t-shirt and pearl necklace grabbing Billy Paul in a bone-crushing hug. "Sports Man Magazine of the Year!" he shouted.

"I like your outfit, Mr. Paulson," Billy smirked, trying to control his trademark cackling laugh, weaving his way through a maze of food tables with its seemingly endless menu: buttered lobster, Shrimp Scampi, Chicken Kiev, deviled eggs stuffed with crème spinach, and five different varieties of salads both fruit and vegetable to roasted pig, and Beef Bundy cooked three different ways. Then there were the gurgling fountains of vodka, gin, scotch, and wine. Beer was abundant in huge tubs of ice.

Two type Three women rushed him, each planting wet kisses on both cheeks. He kissed them in turn, grabbed a beer from a tub, and made his way alone to one of the towering cathedral windows looking past his own reflection in the glass at the not-so-distant lights of Seattle.

Another refection joined him in the glass slowly materializing into sharp focus wearing a smile he hadn't seen...

"Hello Blinkey."

*   *   *

"Good morning, Ms. Farrell," Dan Kaiser greeted, bowing his head slightly as he sat down with his braincase. "It's been a while, Brenda."

"Apparently you two know one another," said Jason Atwater, looking suspiciously over at his corporate attorney.

"Ms. Farrell was one of my fiercest competitors," Kaiser confessed, his eyes a dull, predatory grey. "San Francisco, was it not?"

"D-A's office," said Farrell. "You seem to have gotten smaller."

"Let's get on with it, shall we," Atwater insisted. "I promised you two minutes."

Kaiser reached into his briefcase and removed a blue folder. "I'm here to offer DreamQwest a deal," he said, setting it neatly down on Atwater's desk.

"A deal, Mr. Kaiser?"

"A merger, Jason."

"If I remember correctly we went over this once before. That was six months ago. The verdict's still the same."

Brenda Farrell pushed the blue folder back at Kaiser.

"Why should DreamQwest merge with Virtual World," she said.

"I believe it is in both our interests."

"How so?"

"Both print and network media have raised concerns about recent deaths associated with Big Red."

"Sudden death syndrome has been with us for decades, and probably much farther back than that." said Farrell. "Yes, some people go to bed at night and don't wake up."

"Some of them children, Brenda— most were fully awake wearing Big Reds."

"We stand by our record, Dan."

"A merger with Virtual World will allow DreamQwest to continue creating the games that have proved so popular with customers."

"Under your logo," countered Atwater. "And what about Big Red?"

"Virtual gaming doesn't require one. With few exceptions, many of your games can be converted to a 3-D format to satisfy your customers."

"Wearing 3-D goggles?" Atwater replied. "The very reason our customers chose Big Red."

Dan Kaiser pushed the blue folder back to Brenda Farrell .

"You have been fortunate so far, Jason. I would be careful. What if H-H-S and centers for disease decide a recall is in order?"

CHAPTER TEN

"I'll be honest with you sweetie," said Molly, scrunching her nose, a stethoscope slung around her thick neck. "You don't look good."

"And you're not a doctor," said Kelly, the pain and nausea returning.

"We're going to have to get that infection under control," Molly said, raising Kelly's head slightly. "Open." She shoved some antibiotics into his mouth followed by a glass of water and a large thumb pressed against his lips to make sure he didn't spit them out.

"You smell, sweetie. I'm gonna have to wash you."

"Over my dead body!" said Kelly trying to catch his breath.

"You just might get your wish, sweetie."

*   *   *

"Eyes are open," the coroner said, removing the Big Red and handing it to the detective. "Collar deflated normally."

"Relatives been notified?"

"Neighbor says his son's a patient over at the V-A hospital."

The coroner snapped off his gloves. "Can't really say. Won't know until I I run some tests and get him on the table."

*   *   *

Brenda Farrell was sitting in a chair half asleep when Kelly opened his eyes. "She almost drowned me, you know," he groaned.

"Mom's known Molly for years," said Brenda, touching lightly Kelly's fresh bandages. "Temperature's down. I think you're going to make it."

"I'll let you know in the morning," Kelly groaned. "Right now I feel like—"

"Need a bedpan?"

"A couple weeks ago when I was all normal you couldn't stand the sound of my voice and now you're offering me a bedpan."

"That's because you came across as an arrogant self-centered asshole."

"What's changed?"

"We'll leave it go at that." Farrell's eyes turned inward. "I told Jason about that idea you had regarding Eleanor Chapman."

"It wasn't my idea. I remember what Ben Nettlebaum said at the last meeting."

"Jason agreed. No attorneys. Just Mrs. Chapman. A full examination of her husband's Big Red. Depending on what we find, a cash settlement in compensation for her loss."

"Did she—?"

"No response so far."

Kelly swung his legs painfully over the side of the cot.

"What are you doing?"

"Back's bothering me." Kelly held on to the cot as his feet hit the floor. "Damn that's cold."

Farrell helped him into his slippers. "Think you can make it downstairs?"

"How long was I out?"

"Thanksgiving was two days ago. Hope you like leftovers."

*   *   *

The Ohio Director of Veterans Affairs took one look at the letter on his desk and hit the intercom. "Mitch. Get hold of Pennetta in Cleveland. I'm sending him a copy of a letter I just received. I want to know the circumstances surrounding the death of retired Staff Sergeant Clarence Middleton this past weekend. I want some answers."

The staff sergeant in question was thirty-three. He had served in Afghanistan in 2025. The letter was from his wife explaining her husband's depression caused him to take up gaming. He was found deceased in his room wearing a Big Red"

*　　　*　　　*

Lots of people played games on their tablets, smart phones, and laptops. In his case it was a Big Red. According to Middleton's health records and notes, he'd been getting the best psychiatric care possible at the Cleveland Clinic for the past several years.

"I'll take care of it right away, sir."

The staff sergeant however wasn't the first. The list was still growing.

"I have some good news. The D-O-J finished its investigation. You've been cleared of collusion, obstruction of justice, and misrepresenting federal authority," said Farrell, sneaking a glance in Kelly's direction. "You'll be officially notified by mail."

"Oh. How wonderful!" Kimberly gushed, patting her hands together like a little girl. "I hope you're hungry, young man."

"Who do I thank?"

"I believe his name was Arthur Bell."

The dining room and kitchen was one big room with a solid red oak table at its center. It seated six. Mom Kimberly was at the head in her wheelchair. Brenda and Kelly sat to her right. Molly was at the far end, already helping herself to the turkey and filling. The baked yams, gravy, biscuits, and what was left of the big bird along with a couple freshly baked apple and pumpkin pies were at center table. Whipped cream was optional.

Kimberly lowered her head. "Thank you, Lord, for the food we are about to eat. May you bless this house and everyone in it—and may my daughter at last have found her man."

"Mother. Please."

Molly laughed. "Amen."

Kelly hadn't experienced anything like it since leaving home for the Army back in '2010. That was one war and two parents ago. Until now, Billy Paul was the closest relative he had.

"Please tell us," Kimberly said with one eye on her daughter. "What are your plans for the future, young man?"

"Staying out of trouble…"

"That's because you were on your way to dyin'," said Molly. "If you ask me I got here just in time."

"Well, he's staying with us until he gets back on his feet—right daughter?"

"I guess, Mother," said Brenda, shaking her head. "Not long, I hope. He has a job waiting for him at DreamQwest."

Kelly had trouble swallowing his dinner. "When was this?"

"Jason discussed it with me a few days ago."

Kimberly raised her glass of brandy. "Keep it in the family I say."

"I can't. Not right now," Kelly confessed, disappointing his audience. "I need to check on an old friend."

The dining room grew quiet.

"It's there if you want it," said Brenda, in a take-it-or-leave-it tone.

"Look. I appreciate it." he said. "Seriously. There's something I need to take care of first."

"Better dig in," said Molly. "The filling's getting cold."

*   *   *

Senator Bell was busy getting his affairs in order. Thirty years had taken their toll: the late-night sessions, the glad-handing junkets, the political dinners. It got old fast. In the end he realized he hadn't done much of anything significant. Certainly, not what he had hoped for when he first ran for election.

The country had grown lazy, he thought. Indifferent, and cynical.

Too much money in the wrong hands. Humpty Dumpty, he thought, had fallen off the wall and the country seemed unable to put all the pieces back together again.

Part of the reason for DreamQwest Corporation's remarkable success.

Bell took a sip of tonic water. Too bad it didn't have an ounce of gin in it. He missed the drinking; his liver did not. His impending departure from government left him with one regret. His loyal staff, many who had served him well over the years, seemed to be walking around like the living dead, drifting in and out of his senate office in some dreaded dream state. A few would end up getting rehired by his successor. Many of them would not.

"You have a call on four, Senator Bell. It's Congressman Gordon Greene."

"Thank you, Shirley."

"Arthur!" The voice was southern Alabama.

"Afternoon, Gordon."

As Chairman of the Senate Intelligence Committee, Bell couldn't remember the last time they had talked.

"Am I interrupting?"

"Just sitting back with a glass of tonic water over ice thinking what it would be like being an average citizen again."

"You should add some down-home spirits in there. Might as well be water for Heaven's sake."

"Doctor's orders. What can I do for you, Gordon?"

"Just received a communication from the secretary of health and human services. Since May of 2025 statistics show a five percent increase in unexplained deaths not attributed to complications from epilepsy, heart failure, or old age."

"Why are you telling me this?"

"In October 2025, about a year after Big Red entered the market, sudden unexplained deaths began showing up in medical reports. About two percentage points above the national average over previous years. All ages, and not just those with underlying medical problems."

"Statistics can mean whatever you want them to."

"In the first six months of this year the Center for Disease Control re-ported a three percent surge in unexplained deaths among the general population."

Senator Bell set his tonic water down. "Go on."

"Health and Human Services has already released a consumer alert against DreamQwest, Arthur. And the news media running with it."

"Standard procedure."

"They are now recommending a temporary cease and desist order on all production and sale of Big Reds."

Arthur Bell still had to clear out his desk. His official retirement date was still a week away. He also understood what Gordon was say-ing, and what wasn't: DreamQwest had huge military contracts. Combat simulators for all four branches including anti missile systems for the Navy and Air Force. That didn't include advanced electronic technology in the medical sciences, and in education. Whatever affects DreamQwest affects a good portion of the American economy. Too big to fail was not just some hoary political phrase tossed about by politicians running for office.

"It may not stop there, Arthur. If DreamQwest does nothing to improve the situation, I'm afraid they'll be looking at a worldwide recall of Big Red. Enjoy your retirement, Arthur. My best to Emily."

Bell's Quantum peeled off two recent letters from Health and Human Services the moment the conversation ended.

"My Robert was ten. Sometimes he'd wet himself playing that stupid machine. He sometimes missed lunch even when I made something he liked. After school he couldn't wait to get home to play Triassic Hunt. It was his favorite game. Despite everything we did, he'd spend more and more time on that thing. He was becoming an addict. He'd say and do anything to sneak in a few hours. I have no idea what he did when we were asleep. I regret ever buying that thing."

"Edgar was 18. He was a diabetic. We found him still wearing his

*Big Red that morning; he sometimes played all night. We were cleaning
out his room a day or two after the funeral and found his supply of in-
sulin he'd purchased still in his drawer. He had been so absorbed with
that thing he'd forgotten to take them."*

Frank Kelly thought he knew the place. Billy's address had long
since evaporated from his mind. Like so many things, Billy and he
lived different lives. The name of the street wasn't familiar to him,
either. All he knew was that it wasn't too far from the needle: Seattle's
national trademark. The lights of down-town Seattle were now bleed-
ing up into a darkening twilight over the mostly porchfront homes in
this quiet neighborhood. Kelly hoped he got it right.

Christmas lights, inflated snowmen, nativity scenes over-populated
whole lawns with plastic angels and gold trumpets; windows decorated
with green wreaths on red ribboned doors.

It was Christmas in Seattle; at least where Billy Paul lived.

The green-sided detached single home with a jeep in the driveway
caught Kelly's attention. This had to be it, he thought. The jeep was
Billy Paul's for sure on closer inspection.

Kelly hesitated a couple doubts later before mounting the steps
to a familiar front door. He'd been to the house maybe three times
since they started working together in Product Division. He had
called the office from Ann Arbor and again when he landed in
Seattle but got no answer which was strange. Nothing. Not even a
recording. Had Homeland finally pulled the plug on Product
Division?

Kelly hit the bell with the heel of his hand. Failing a response, he
gave a couple pounding knocks.

"What the hell you looking for?" came a phlegm-filled voice from
somewhere behind him. It had age.

Kelly half turned. "I'm looking for—"

"Frank Kelly!" the elderly man shouted, looking down as if trying
to forget something.

"Duncan?"

"Where you been, Frank?"

The barbeque two summers ago in Billy Paul's backyard throwing horseshoes over beer. Duncan, in fact, had beaten them both that evening. Kelly came off the steps to catch his hand.

"You don't know?" Duncan had trouble forming the words. "Billy's gone."

"Gone? His jeep's still—"

Duncan pulled his hand away. "Billy, uh, passed away, Frank. All I know is I hadn't seen him much lately. Knew he wasn't working. Had to call the cops. Had to give 'em my keys—"

Kelly had trouble catching his breath. "When was this?"

"Few nights ago," Duncan said wiping both hands over his face.

"It's okay, Dunk."

"I'm gonna miss him, Kel."

"Does Robbie know?"

"Geez, Frank, It ain't really my place—I couldn't tell him his dad's dead."

CHAPTER ELEVEN

Jason Atwater did what he always did when he disliked what he was reading: he dropped the offending document unceremoniously on his desk.

"Would you care to explain this, Brenda?"

"It's a lawsuit," said Farrell. "Baum, Radcliffe and Jones. Private attorneys. One of the best. The deceased was a child. Age ten. His parents are sparing no effort it seems. Their son was playing Triassic Hunt."

"We've sold over one hundred million devices in thirty-seven countries over the past two years," Atwater said. "That doesn't include thirty million plus right here in the United States since the company's inception in twenty-twenty-four." He looked at Farrell, expecting an answer. "Is there any way we can get access to the boy's Big Red?"

"I wouldn't even try," she said. "What would it prove? Obstruction? Tampering with evidence?"

Atwater folded his hands under his chin as he usually did when he felt insecure. "What are our options?"

"We release a press statement saying we stand by our product."

"Do we?"

*   *   *

Retirement now seemed to be Kelly's best option. He had time in service and age and enough in the bank to pay maybe two month's rent on his Seattle apartment. Kelly had back pay of course, along with unused sick, holiday and vacation time. His first retirement check wouldn't make it to his checking account for at least a month.

One thing he was sure of: He had the DreamQwest job if he wanted it. He knew he could do it skateboarding on one leg. How hard could it be anyway? Out in the middle of nowhere. Surrounded by three thousand acres of lakes and rolling forest. He couldn't imagine anyone showing up with criminal intent. In-house crime had to be pretty much nonexistent. DreamQwest was a virtual corporate Fort Knox.

Arrangements were made to fly him out for his meeting with Boy Wonder. Yet he couldn't quite see himself in a security manager's role. He couldn't see himself as another Richard Head. At least in Product Division there was always the remote possibility he'd find an actual terrorist device.

"I'm assuming you heard," said Brenda as Kelly threw his backpack in the back of Brenda's Mercedes.

"I caught the news at the airport. They're making you guys out to look like a House of Horrors."

"More and more cases are being reported," she complained. "I don't know what to make of it."

"Big Red didn't actually hit the market until twenty-five. That's three years ago. How come it's a problem now?" said Kelly.

"More people are discovering what it can do. More games. More scenario building. Then there's sharing. That's the new craze."

"What about enemies?"

"Enemies?"

"Don't pretend you don't have any. Jason didn't get this far without pissing off a few people."

"Well, there's our competition, Virtual World—"

"Politicians maybe?"

"There isn't a politician living today he hasn't helped in some way."

"What about Ben?"

"What about him?"

Kelly laughed. "You have to be kidding. He made the damn thing.

If anyone knows how to fix the problem it's him."

"Look what he's done," Farrell said, with pride in her voice. "The Ultra system for starters. He's making a series of programs on historical figures so children can get to meet and talk with people like Shakespeare, Julius Caesar, Neil Armstrong, Martin Luther King..."

Farrell's re-focused her attention on the roadway as they merged onto Atwater Drive. "By the way. You have an appointment with Human Resources."

"What for?"

"All new hires have to go through orientation."

*   *   *

"The Federal Communications Commission officially requested our records," said Atwater. "They've put out an advisory. Our Asian and European partners are under similar regulations."

"I want this understood," Atwater said, his voice rising. "There will be no layoffs—."

The doors to the office opened.

"What's this about layoffs?" said Kelly, waving a set of papers in both hands. "I just went through a four hour puppet show without no-doze and you guys are talking layoffs."

"Unfortunately, it is part of doing business on occasion," Atwater replied stoically. "Please take a seat, Frank."

"Look, I can survive on my what I have—"

"You will do nothing of the kind!" Atwater snapped, reaching into his desk drawer, pulling out a worn hardbound book, setting it down on the desk. "My grandfather's first book: Holographic Reality. It explains all you need to know about the science behind Big Red. I will arrange a meeting with Ben Nettlebaum if you need additional help understanding it."

Kelly had read parts of it years ago in college. It was the craze then, though mostly required reading with among the fraternities.

"Is there going to be a quiz?"

"This," he said, handing Kelly an embossed metallic card, "will open any door anywhere on DreamQwest property. As our security manager you will need it."

"Right now, I'm staying at the Radnor Lakeside—"

"Not anymore. Your official residence is here in Tower One," said Atwater. "Get situated. Make sure you read the book. Lieutenant Finney will be waiting to take you to your new home. I expect to see you bright and early tomorrow morning."

"Got it."

A familiar figure stood waiting in the lobby as Kelly stepped off the elevator.

"Didn't see you this morning when I came in," said Kelly.

"I hear you got the job, sir," said the big guard. "Congratulations, sir. I'm supposed to take you to your new living quarters."

"Special forces?"

"Sir—?"

"I noticed the taboo on your neck."

"Seals, sir."

"I was close."

"Your baggage, sir?"

"Just this." Kelly held up his backpack. "The rest of my things should be here in about a week."

"I'll advise the men, sir."

"Uh, Finney. Look. Drop the sir stuff. The name's Frank."

"You're my boss, sir," he said, the stoic acceptance on his wide, rugged face remained unchanged. "Your apartment's around back, sir."

"Apartment."

"Yes, sir."

Kelly followed Finney to the rear of Tower One. It had no address. No indication it was anything more than the base of Tower One's metallic blue-grey exterior. There were no windows, or a door that he could see.

"Did Mr. Atwater assign you an access card, sir?"

"Uh, yeah." Kelly removed his card and handed it to Finney. "See that slot sir?"

"Barely."

"It's brighter at night, sir." Finny flipped the card over. "Fingerprint side, sir."

A seamless section of the exterior opened.

"It will close automatically when you enter, sir," said Finney, returning his card.

"Anything else I need to know?"

"Your weapon, sir." Finney reached for something behind his back and came out with a black leather clip-on holster with a Sig Sauer tucked inside. "And a full fourteen round clip, sir"

"I'm starting to feel at home, now."

"Let me show you around, sir."

The living room alone was larger than his apartment in Seattle.

It came with a 60-inch wall-mounted flat screen above a gas-heated fireplace, a floor-to-ceiling library waiting for books to fill it, a huge armchair, two full couches, a huge glass coffee table, and a desk with a Quantum, all resting on an expensive grey shag carpet.

The bathroom would have been huge even without the Jacuzzi. The kitchen/dining room combination included a fully stocked refrigerator-freezer along with coffee maker, and microwave.

The bedroom came equipped with a similar bathroom along with a 60-inch TV.

"Eighteen hundred square feet, sir."

"Don't they have anything smaller?"

"This is the smallest we have, sir," said Finney, "If you have any questions, there's a number on the back where you can reach me, sir."

"Is this normal?"

"I'm in Tower Four—that's security, maintenance and engineering. Just across the concourse from Tower One, sir."

"This is the basic unit."

"Yes, sir. Family units are larger—one hundred and twenty of them to be exact. All but three are occupied. The complex itself has two supermarkets, eight retail shops, three Olympic size pools over by the fountain area, and two indoor parks just behind Tower Three. A detailed map is available on your Ultra, sir."

"I'll be spending most of my time cleaning this place," Kelly complained.

"We have in-house services, sir. Number's on your Ultra. Ms. Farrell, our corporate attorney, occupied this one for a time."

"You're kidding."

"It wasn't long. Her mother suffered a stroke about a year and a half ago. They were offered one of our larger units, but Ms. Farrell's mother didn't want to give up her house, or her cats, sir."

"She commutes."

"Yes, sir. The only one who does. I'll let you go. Have a nice evening, sir."

"Ahh, one last question, Finney. Has anyone ever quit?"

"Quit, sir?"

"Resigned their employment."

"No one I can remember, sir."

*   *   *

Kelly stayed in his suite that night trying to get through the first few chapters of the book Atwater had given him. It wasn't an easy read. He failed physics in high school and wasn't much better in college. He had a basic idea of what Big Red did for a living.

The introduction to the book gave him goose bumps:

"If people could enter the world of dreams of their choosing to work out their problems, their fantasies, their aggressions, the world would be a better place free of wars and crimes against humanity; a world of civil harmony where everyone was equal in the eyes of another. Creating a Heaven where none existed before."

Most gamers knew enough to configure a game, and that was it. Of course, he didn't think the book would help much. Kelly had forgotten most of what he learned about Quantum mechanics, or string theory, or 3-D printing for that matter. Kelly didn't fail physics; physics failed Kelly.

Virtual Reality, Big Red's major competition, was a less complicated gaming system and had been around for decades All a player needed was a game and a pair of ungainly goggles one strapped to their head and react to a particular scenario, whether it was golfing, or hand-to-hand combat, or blasting opposing alien forces with particle guns like he did in college. Easy and simple, though never quite realistic. It also helped if you were athletic. The clumsy and uncoordinated should at least have medical insurance.

DreamQwest was daylight as Virtual World was to night.

Big Red required only the comfort of one's home, a chair, bed, or couch, and no one had to jump around reacting to whatever the game threw at you. In Big Red, according to what he learned in Human Resources, the scenarios in DreamQwest were indistinguishable from reality, the player fully immersed in an unscripted scenario of one's own creation. Like Brenda Farrell's confrontation with an African Rhino was a prime example of how real it could be.

The new craze was scenario sharing.

Until the Marcy Collins case, no one had ever died using a Big Red. Kelly could not find any plausible number of reasons why Marcy Collins should have died in her own apartment sitting on her own couch in her own living room without some underlying medical condition.

But what if that was the case?

Did a person need to be medically cleared to ride a roller coaster at an amusement park? Or drink all night at the corner bar with friends?

That might be something to bring up at the next meeting.

Ben Nettlebaum was the go-to guy since he was the prime developer of Two-Seven-Five; the enhancer that made the game as popular as it was. One thing Kelly learned over his relatively short lifetime was that brilliant people had a tendency of insulating themselves from their own arrogance; possibly the reason why the Titanic had so few lifeboats since the ship was thought to be unsinkable.

Nothing and no one was infallible. Sure, there were disclaimers and product warning labels to protect companies against misuse of their products. Kelly was certain DreamQwest had one as well.

Marcy Collins was in apparent good health when she crawled inside her Big Red.

The problem was she didn't crawl back out.

It might not have been obvious to anyone, or even her supposed lover, that it was even possible to have in-game sex. Kelly had never had a vivid dream that he was aware of.

Dreaming of having a love affair with your neighbor's wife or husband was not a crime.

Unlike reality, Collins' alleged romantic encounter with Peter Chapman, if were ever found to be true, had no basis in law. That his wife had accused her husband of infidelity based on his addiction to DreamQwest was laughable. The fact she herself did not own a Big Red made it totally laughable.

Most companies now had game rooms, and emporiums. Libraries now featured them as well. Games could be played almost anywhere on lunch break. All that was needed was a Big Red and a network. Chapman and Collins, separated by well over a thousand miles was no different than a spouse sneaking a peak at an x-rated movie.

Marcy Collins, the federal attorney for the state of Illinois, apparently enjoyed her time off. She lived alone with nothing more than a Big Red for company. It was a game after all. It also came with its own built-in computer called a Quantum. Apparently, owning a Big Red was all one needed for a fun time.

Unlike computer files, telephone bills, or emails, in the commission of a crime, there was no way anyone could know what anyone was doing once in game, or that you or anyone else was having an affair? Did anyone even care what anyone did on Big Red?

Law enforcement agencies relied on warrants based on probable cause to obtain records, like cell phone bills and other forms of traceable, public domain forms of communication; and if not, warrants. Big Red was a computer-based gaming system regulated by the Federal Communications Commission only because of Big Red's ability to network. Like electronic toys, Big Red left no record of use as to who played with whom or didn't on any given day. Scenarios could be erased.

From the brief conversation Kelly had with Eleanor Chapman, it didn't take a lot of imagination to know, like millions of others, that many of Washington's social elite had Big Reds, and possibly for the same reason her husband did. Eleanor was a career government wife after all and played by the same rules whether she liked those rules or not.

Only the outcome didn't fit the script.

CHAPTER TWELVE

Kelly made his way to the front of Tower One short of a good night's sleep. He was looking forward to a good cup of coffee in the corporate cafeteria one level above Human Resources. Maybe he'd get Lieutenant Finney to show him the rest of the DreamQwest complex.

He rounded the main entrance when four shuttles converged on the tower at about the same time his Ultra sounded. One of them was Lieutenant Finney and three of his guards at about the same time Kelly's Ultra sounded.

"Kelly."

"We have a problem up in the penthouse, sir."

"I'm approaching the lobby," he said as Finney and his men spilled out of their shuttles. A yellow and white paramedic van, lights flashing, came up between them.

Two of the guards took up position in front of the entrance armed with shotguns.

"What's going on?" Kelly wanted to know.

"It's the office, sir," said Finney hitting the top button with the heal of his big hand.

"Atwater?"

"Don't know," said Finney, as the elevator doors opened. Both noticed the huge doors leading to the office at the end of the corridor were open.

Finney unholstered his sidearm and slowly approached the office.

"Permit me, sir," he said, holding Kelly back, shielding him with his huge body. They found the office empty. Nothing appeared out of place.

Kelly noticed the restroom door at the back of the office slightly ajar. Finney kicked it open, his weapon at the ready.

They found Ben Nettlebaum lying face down on the floor, Jason Atwater keeling beside, shaking his head with one hand palm-down on his back.

"He's not breathing," said Atwater, eyes red with tears.

"Paramedics are on their way, sir," said Finney,

"What happened?" said Kelly.

"Said he had to use the... restroom," Atwater explained "When he didn't come out..."

"How long?"

"Half an hour maybe."

"Secure the lobby," Finney ordered over his Ultra. "No one is to leave or enter the building. Paramedics only."

Kelly helped Jason to his feet. "He was fine when he came to the office," said Atwater. "He seemed tired."

"We have to clear the bathroom," said Finney. "They're here, sir."

The paramedics banged their way into the bathroom as they maneuvered a stretcher through the narrow doorway off-loading medical equipment on the way in.

Kelly's Ultra issued an alert. It was Farrell.

"What's going on? I tried calling the office—"

"Where are you?"

"Atwater Drive. "

"Listen—"

"Where's Jason?" He called me half hour ago. I couldn't understand what he was saying."

"It's Ben, Brenda—"

The paramedics pushed their way out with Ben Nettlebaum strapped to a stretcher, his face ashen, body stiff and lifeless. One of them handed

Kelly a pair of thick-lensed glasses and shook his head negatively.

I'll explain when you get here."

"Are all these guns necessary!" Brenda Farrell shouted the moment she arrived.

Atwater was at his desk, shaken, disheveled with grief, gripping a cup of coffee with total disinterest.

"It's procedure, Ms. Farrell," said Finney, excusing himself. "I'll take care of it."

"What's going on?" she wanted to know.

"Ben's dead," said Kelly.

"We have lost a member of the family," Atwater said in his own way. "He was my professor at Alameda," he continued. "Post graduate studies in theoretical physics at Cal-Tech in artificial intelligence, and..."

Brenda rounded the desk and embraced him from behind. "Oh, Jason, I'm so sorry."

"Ben and I formed a company called Galaxy Qwest after my crooked father passed on, leaving me with the fruits of his ill-gotten schemes. Ben and I developed the next generation technology for a variety of gaming companies: Virtual World was one of them."

Brenda Farrell straightened. "I never knew that."

"Need to know my beautiful Brenda," he said, a twisted smile cracking his boyish lips, not knowing whether to laugh or cry. "In any case we sold our interests and began development of a whole new concept called Dream-Qwest."

"I think you need a beer," said Kelly.

Atwater, limp in his chair, looked at him accusingly. "You know, Frank. That is one beverage I have never had the desire to experience."

"It's, well...a matter of taste."

"Which you don't have," said Farrell, taking a call on her Ultra. It was Dan Kaiser, Chapman's attorney. She put it on audio and set it down on the desk so everyone could hear.

"*Brenda.*"

"We're all listening, Dan."

"Eleanor Chapman would like to arrange a meeting at your earliest convenience regarding her case."

"I thought I postponed that once before— "

"My client was rather impressed with Mr. Kelly during an encounter they recently shared in Washington, if I'm not mistaken."

Brenda glanced over at Kelly for authentication. Kelly confirmed it with a quick nod. "It was after the shooting…"

"What about Thursday. Ten o'clock. Your office."

Atwater quietly agreed. "Tell him that's fine."

"Ten o'clock. Yes. Agreed," said Farrell as the call disconnected.

"You never mentioned having met Eleanor Chapman."

"I wasn't expecting it. She came into my room at the hospital with issues. Hated the whole world. Suspected her husband of having an affair."

"Was he?" Atwater asked.

"How would I know? Chapman was nothing more than a voice over the phone."

"It must have been something you said—"

"I was in the hospital flat on my back with tubes sticking out of every orifice . She hated the fact her husband was dead. Hate does something to a person sometimes."

"So what did you do?" asked Farrell.

"I told her DreamQwest might be able to help."

*   *   *

Atwater was making arrangements with Ben's family and carry out his wish to be cremated when Martin Smyth requested a meeting. That it was urgent.

"This better be good, Martin."

"I found something of interest you might want to see," said Smyth, assuming all lab duties in the wake of Ben's death. "It might be worth your time, sir."

"It's a data disc," said Atwater, unsure at first what Smyth was trying to tell him.

"The one from Collins' Big Red, sir. The one Agent Kelly brought us."

"The one with nothing on it."

"I believe he forgot to put it back, sir."

"That doesn't sound like Ben."

"No, sir. But I think I know why. There are DreamQwest mechanize centers all across the country. They maintain records on all exchanges, defective data discs, and Big Reds returned for one reason or another. The serial numbers on this disc do not match."

"How do you know that?"

"I checked. The bar code on this one doesn't match."

"The one Kelly brought us."

"Yes, sir. It was a blank."

"So what are you telling me?"

"Whoever did this replaced Collins' data disc with a blank purchased from a store Maryland."

"Maryland?"

"Whoever switched Collins' disc exchanged it with a blank."

"And the real one?"

"It was exchanged. That means the Maryland store has Collins' original data disc. It's company policy that any defective or returned parts are kept for ninety days. After that the returned discs are destroyed."

"And the Big Red's?"

"They're refurbished and resold with new discs."

"I want Collins' original data disc," said Atwater. "I want you to go to Maryland personally to pick it up."

"Yes, but..."

"I'll authorize it."

"Mr. Kelly," Eleanor Chapman said, stepping away from her attorney long enough to get close to him. There was no veil this time. Behind the clear eyes dry of pain reflected a rather handsome middle-aged woman. The long velvet coat she wore covered most of her down to her black leather boots.

"You seem to have recovered well," she said, looking directly into Kelly's eyes.

"Eleanor."

"Shall we," said Atwater, stepping between them, leading them down the same corridor he had traveled before with Ben Nettlebaum. Dan Kaiser, her attorney, was close behind with his briefcase.

Brenda Farrell had been cool to the idea at first. She didn't think much of the meeting since it gave Dan Kaiser a possible advantage in any court proceedings. One thing she learned from experience was never reveal your hand to a practiced opponent the likes of Dan Kaiser; a veteran of many court battles, well-known for his numerous victories.

Dan Kaiser also personally knew a lot of damn good judges.

Brenda Farrell wanted to establish some rules. Although Eleanor Chapman's grief was understandable, DreamQwest was only a game. In any case, no one was really sure, including how the proceeding was going to turn out. In a way, she almost dreaded the thought of finding out.

Eleanor Chapman had indeed lost her husband, but if DreamQwest was somehow the cause of so much hurt, Atwater would make it right.

Martin Smyth, the balding middle-aged scientist who inherited Ben Nettlebaum's position as lead scientist, had returned that morning from the DreamQwest store in Maryland with Collins' original data disc the morning she was found deceased in her Chicago penthouse.

Atwater made sure there were plenty of chairs: two new plush chairs in addition to the four in his office. A rather large monitor was set up facing the chairs, along with a table that offered coffee, tea, and milk and a tray of sandwiches. Atwater had his own tray with the customary chocolate donut holes and a large glass of milk.

Eleanor Chapman and Kaiser sat closest facing the monitor.

"Are there any questions before we start?" said Farrell, taking a chair next to Kelly nearest Atwater's desk.

"What? No popcorn?" Kelly whispered.

"Where is the Big Red?" Kaiser asked, setting his briefcase down next to his chair.

"Collins' Big Red is in federal custody at the moment," said Farrell. "You will understand at the end of our briefing the reason for it."

Atwater nodded his approval. "You may begin, Martin."

"Thank you, sir," said Smyth.

"In my hand is the original data disc from Collins' Big Red," Smyth said, holding up a gold-plated disc in full view of everyone in the room.

"How do we know that's from Marcy Collins' Big Red?" said Kaiser.

"Our lead scientist, Martin Smyth," Atwater explained. "He returned just this morning from one of our DreamQwest stores located in Maryland with Marcy Collins' original data disc taken from her Big Red.

Smyth walked over to the large projection screen and inserted the disc into the first of two slots.

The lights in the office dimmed.

The image steadied showing a crowded open-air market with crude stalls displaying merchandise as the image of three guitar-strumming Mexicans singing *Ranchero* dressed in typical broad-rimmed black and gold hats performing to a crowd of camera-wielding tourists.

"*Ole! Ole!*" a young woman shouted from a crowd in Cancun, Mexico, an attractive sunlit face warm with too many beers, singing, dancing as best she could beside a man everyone in Atwater's office recognized.

"Is that who I think it is?" said Dan Kaiser, leaning forward in his chair for a closer look. "It's Dirk Crawford."

"President Crawford."

"They're scenario sharing," said Farrell. "Our customers do it all the time. Dreaming isn't exactly a crime."

"It's still cheating," said Eleanor Chapman.

Frank Kelly explained it differently. "It was your husband who ordered me to Chicago. Chapman ordered me to pick it up from F-B-I custody and bring it to him in Washington."

"What happened?" said Kaiser.

"Went to Chicago as ordered. Alec Farris was the agent in charge of the scene. Said he was told to leave the Big Red at evidence custodian in Chicago for pickup."

Kaiser laughed. "How convenient."

"When Kelly brought it to us as requested, we discovered the original data disc had been replaced with a blank."

"What about my husband?" said Eleanor Chapman. "They told me he committed suicide."

"What about Marcy Collins?" said Kelly.

Atwater took in a deep breath. "The perfect crime."